Thanks as always go to my wife, Laura, who's murderous mind I rely on daily! None of these books would have been possible without you xx
This book is for my mum, thank you for all you have done.

Contents

Chapter 1

Four years ago.....

Ellie is driving along Great Western Road, the snow is falling and drivers are taking it a bit slower on this cold January night. She is singing along to Take That on the radio when her phone started to ring through the speakers.

"This better be good because you just interrupted the chorus of 'Never Forget'" she said down the phone as she heard Gavin chuckling.

"Of all guilty pleasures to choose, you go for Take That...mental...anyway I'm just calling to say that I've picked up the pizzas and I'm on my way to yours now."

"Cool, I'm nearly home so I'll meet you there. You ready to watch your team get humped?" she joked. Ever since she took the job as DI in the Serious Crime unit, she had formed a bond with her DC Gavin Bickerton, especially when she found out they had a shared passion for the NFL and tonight, both of their teams were playing each other for a place in the Superbowl.

"You wish, Brady is too old now, no way he'll make it to another Superbowl win. We need tonight mate, after this week, just to unwind before we need to go back to the manhunt." Gavin said earnestly. Half of the Glasgow force was currently out looking for John Peter Cotton, a man suspected of multiple murders and who Ellie had been instrumental in profiling.

"We'll catch him, it's just a matter of time. Hopefully no one else gets hurt before we get him." Ellie said as she pulled the car to a slippery stop outside her flat. "That's me home Gav, I'll get the telly on and some plates ready."

"Plates? What are you 80? Who uses plates for pizza?"

"Shut up and excuse me for trying to teach you some etiquette before your wedding. See you in a few." she hung up and got out of the car, the frosty air cutting at her face as she walked gingerly along the path and towards her door. The street light flickered as she made her way up the steps, she felt the presence before she heard anything. An arm tightened around her throat and a heavy body pressed her against her own front door. She smelled his breath as he whispered in her ear, "I will walk among you. I will be your God. And you will be my people." Ellie struggled but his heavier weight kept her pinned as he grabbed her left hand and slammed it against the door as he continued his bible verses. "You will hunt down your enemies. You will kill them with your swords". Panic was rising in Ellie as she used all her strength to push against what she knew was coming, she had seen his handiwork in images and at crime scenes for weeks. She tried kicking back to sweep his legs but she missed and was rewarded with a kick to the back of her knee that sent her forwards and down on her knees, her head smacked hard against the metal letterbox on the door and it left her dazed as she felt blood running down her face. It was only when she felt the pierce of sharp metal against her hand that her focus returned along with her panic as he drove the large nail through the middle of her hand and into the door. Pain seared through her as she let out a scream that she never knew she was capable of. Her brain couldn't make sense of anything anymore, she felt a horrible burning pain and nothing else. She vaguely heard yelling and a scuffle behind her as her head started swimming. Still nailed to the door, she managed to turn her head enough to see two people fighting, blood stinging her eyes. Gavin had arrived and had launched himself forward pinning Cotton to the ground and shouted her name, it was the last thing she heard before everything went black.

Chapter 2

Present Day...

The family are still all gathered in Ellie and Kate's living room after the shock of the letter received. Gavin is pacing, waiting on the Chief to call back about Cottons whereabouts. Kate was holding Ellie's hand as she had remained pale and quiet ever since the letter arrived for her, she was still holding the Tarot card in her other hand. Peggy had been watching from her position on the sofa and decided Ellie needed to talk this through.

"Ellie, who is Cotton and what does he want with you?"

Ellie sighed and looked up at the older woman who had the sympathetic eyes of someone who had faced fear eye to eye. Ellie nodded and took a deep breath, Gavin had stopped pacing and had sat down opposite Ellie, he ran his hand though his hair for something to do and then resumed his pacing like a trapped lion.

"John Peter Cotton is a serial killer." Ellie began.

"He was my first murder case as DI when I joined the Serious Crime squad four years ago. He killed six people, that we know of, each victim was found in a graveyard and they were either nailed to a tree...um...crucified for want of a better description, or hanging from cross shaped headstones. Cause of death for each one was manual strangulation or blood loss due to a stab wound around the heart. None of the victims were linked in any way that we could find, all were different ages, genders, and socio-economic backgrounds. I studied him and his crime scenes to build up a profile of him. I said he would be white, in his 30s or early 40s and a loner. He would live quietly either alone or with an elderly relative who he would be cherished by as a good man. I thought that he would come across as deeply religious but will have warped the true interpretation of biblical teachings to his own agenda." Ellie stopped and rubbed at the scar on the back of her hand, remembering just how accurate that initial profile actually was. Gavin carried on the tale as she seemed lost in her thoughts.

"Ellie realised that a killer with religious mania would have chosen his victims for a reason and started to look into their lives. The first victim was an investment banker who squandered millions on cocaine and booze, the next two victims were local sex workers who worked Wellington Street in the city centre, the next man had a previous conviction for beating his ex-wife and the last victim was a woman having an affair with her kids karate teacher. Ellie realised that each of them was a 'sinner' in Cotton's warped mind and his manner of killing was like some sort of biblical judgement on them."

He seemed to miss the whole forgiveness thing in the new testament then?" Aggie asked quietly as Gavin nodded grimly.

"These fanatics always seem to miss that bit" Aggie said in disgust. "How did you catch him?"

"Ellie took a risk and spoke to the press. She did a piece on the local news appealing for information and to give details of the profile of this killer. She described the type of man that the killer would be. The hotline went mental with people eager to help, four people all called with the same name, John Peter Cotton. He had worked as IT support in an office in the city centre and had creeped out the younger women in the office by quoting scripture at them when they would discuss their weekend plans. Two of the lassies had called in to name him. One of them said she had left the job because he cornered her at the bus stop one night and tried to pray for her soul."

"That was genius Ellie, just like Crimewatch. What happened then?" Ann asked.

We went to his house to speak to him but he wasn't

there. His aunt lived with him and she let the team in, said Cotton had gone to church although she couldn't remember what one. We had a quick look around and found a proper serial killer wall in his room, filled with pictures of the victims and newspaper clippings of the killings. There were loads of crosses nailed to the walls with red nails. We knew it was him, we left a patrol outside his house in case he came back and issued an alert for his arrest...then we waited..." Gavin paused and looked towards Ellie with a sad smile, she nodded for him to continue.

"We...um...we decided to have a night off Els and me...I was coming round to watch the Superbowl playoff, didn't think the nutter would do anything on a Sunday you see...Ellie arrived a few minutes before me and was to get the telly on. I got there and I heard screaming...I ran towards her door and found Cotton pinning her to the door...he had um...nailed her hand to it..." he stopped as Aggie and Ann both gasped in horror, tears in their eyes and Peggy sighed sadly and shook her head.

"You never told us..." Ann said quietly as tears fell from her eyes.

"I couldn't..." Ellie responded with a small shrug.

Gavin carried on, a bit quieter now "I ran towards them, Cotton didn't notice me, he was too busy quoting random bits of scripture at Ellie as he choked her with his arm. I tackled him and got him cuffed, Ellie passed out from a head wound and the pain from her hand. I called for backup and an ambulance, Cotton went mad, thrashing about and quoting loads of stuff that I didn't understand. Ellie went to hospital where by luck, she suffered no lasting nerve damage. The nail had missed the major tendons in her hand." Gavin seemed to be at the end of his tale, Kate realised that she had been holding Ellie's hand so tightly that both of their knuckles were white. Ellie smiled at her reassuringly, she had regained some of her colour now that the initial shock had gone.

"What's the tarot card all about though love?" Bill asked with a croaky voice.

"He left one on every victim" Ellie explained. "We never released that fact to the press. I still don't know why he left them, always the death card. My theory is that he saw himself as God's executioner. He didn't realise that the death card in tarot doesn't actually represent death rather change. It was an arrogant challenge to us possibly."

Ann and Aggie had heard enough and had both come to sit by Ellie and give her a reassuring hug. She appreciated these maternal touches more than she could express.

"So what happened to him?" Kate asked Gavin but it was Ellie who answered.

"Well he pled guilty so there was no trial as such, he was proud of his work. He was sentenced to a whole life order to be served at Barlinnie." Ellie explained as Gavin's phone rang. He had forgotten about waiting on a call and jumped when it went off.

"DI Bickerton" he answered clutching at his heart and was silent for a few moments as the person on the other end of the call explained something to him.

"Are you sure Sir? Ok…I'll let her know." He hung up and turned to face Ellie who was expecting to hear terrible news.

"He's dead Els, he died at Barlinnie four days ago. It can't be him."

Chapter 3

Ellie walked into the office the next morning after a restful sleep, knowing that Cotton was dead had lifted a weight from her shoulders that she didn't know she was carrying. Her dad and Aunt Ann had offered to postpone their trip and stay on for a while but she shouted them down and told them not to worry and that they should go on as planned. She had waived them off an hour ago and missed them already.

"Morning boss" chirped Alex Harris as Ellie sat at her desk.

"Morning Ma'am" Sara Kent said with a smile.

"Morning all, have we got anything interesting in?" Ellie asked as she logged her PC on and Harris brought her a coffee.

"Only news from court if you want to hear the gossip?" Harris was bursting to tell her, he was almost doing his version of a 'don't pee' dance.

"What's the goss?" Ellie asked, knowing from the look on his face that it was juicy.

"Well boss I'm sure you know that your new Aunt-in-law Val was due in court this week for Zsa-Zsaing the police officer that came to take some evidence from her house?"

"Uh huh" Ellie murmured. She thought his turn of phrase more glamorous than Auntie Val slapping an officer in the face but Harris loved to guild the lily.

"Well it was this morning, first thing Boss, she got Community Service." Harris said gleefully. "The judge recommended that her time be spent litter picking around her estate." Ellie burst out laughing.

"Oh that will go down well with her, picking up crisp packets and beer bottles alongside the wee neds that joyride. Oh she won't be able to look the neighbourhood watch in the face again." It was the latest in a string of embarrassment for Val, Peggy had it on good authority that she had been asked to resign from the Rotary club committee, the shame!

Ellie appreciated the light jovial gossip, she knew that Gavin will have briefed them before she arrived about the events the day before. This attempt to lighten her mood meant a lot to her.

"So I assume you all heard about the theatrics that went on at my house yesterday?" she asked.

"Yes boss...we heard..." Kent said with a sad smile.

"Well if Cotton is dead I still have questions that need answers, in particular the delivery of the death tarot card to me. That particular piece of Cotton's M.O. was never disclosed to anyone outside the investigation team. Therefore whoever sent it to me has details of his crimes that could only have come from the old team, or from Cotton himself. If we take it that the team haven't been indiscreet as the only members still being around are myself, Gavin, and the Chief as he was the Chief Super back then, why would Cotton talk to anyone about his crimes…and to what end? The tarot card is on its way to forensics to be printed but I want to cover all bases here just in case that this little joke doesn't stop with love letters to my house. Harris can you get on to Barlinnie, I want the files on Cotton from his time there. I want any cell mates, regular visitors, anyone that he struck up a friendship with. I doubt this will be a big list, he wasn't popular on remand if memory serves. Also could you get his medical records from them too? Cotton was not an old man, how did he die? Kent I'd like you to…" the rest of what Ellie was about to say was interrupted by her phone ringing.

"McVey" she answered.

"Ellie" it was the Chief and he sounded serious. "I need you to come to a crime scene."

"Of course Sir, what information do we have?" Ellie asked as she grabbed a pen from her desk to take notes.

"Well…uh…here's the thing Ellie…there was a body found this morning but was found by Inspector Mills. You remember Mills don't you?"

"Of course Sir, he was brought in to advise in the Cotton murders." Ellie had a feeling of dread not helped by the Chief's reluctance to get to the point.

"Well Mills was up visiting his mother this morning…I mean he visited her grave as it would have been her birthday…he found a body near her in the graveyard…this body was nailed to a tree by the hands, a cross nailed above them."

"I see…was there a card?" Ellie asked, dread in the pit of her stomach.

"Yes… Mills found a Tarot card in the victims jacket pocket when he searched for ID. He hasn't touched the body or moved it, he knows better but when he saw the card he called me directly knowing the implications. I've got forensics and uniform down already to secure the scene and take Mills statement but I need you down there."

"I'll go now, what graveyard is it?"

"Western Necropolis, use the main entrance in Cadder and follow the road up to the roundabout and swing right, you'll see the forensics team up there.

"Sir" she acknowledged and hung up the call.

"Gav, we have a body to go see and a potential copycat on our hands." Ellie said as she grabbed her car keys.

Chapter 4

Ellie drove through the wrought iron gates of the main entrance to the Western Necropolis, the city of the dead spanning acres of the north of Glasgow. The press were already at the gates, being held back by the local police cordon. She had no idea how or why they had made it there before her. She had been to a few funerals up here and as much as she loved the beauty of the Victorian graves, today they seemed foreboding. At the top of the hill they parked beside the Doc's car and the forensics van. The wind whipped Ellies hair around her face as they walked toward the white tent and screens behind the row of gravestones ahead of them.

"How the hell did the press find out?" growled Gavin as he stamped his feet to warm them up.

"No idea, someone has been indiscreet would be my guess."

"Are you ok with all this Els? I mean…if you need to take a step back on this case…I wouldn't blame you." Gavin said gently.

"Thanks...but I'm ok. I had a lot of counselling after Cotton, I've come to terms with what happened. If there is some sick bastard fan-girling over him then I'm making sure he causes as little pain as possible. Come on, let's see what the Doc has for us."

Doc Brett heard their voices and had opened the flap in the tent to allow them access.

"What have we got Doc?" Ellie asked quietly, she glanced briefly at the body in-situ before focusing back on the Doc.

"Male victim, mid 50s, I think the local PCs have his ID somewhere and are tracking down next of kin or something. This is the immediate crime scene, from the blood splatters it looks like he was killed here rather than elsewhere. I'll know more once I post him but initial cause of death I would say was heart failure due to his body going into shock."

"Was he...um...is it the same as..." Ellie didn't finish the question but the Doc knew what she was asking. She squeezed her hand as she answered.

"Yes Ellie, it's the same, large nails have been driven through his hands into the tree bark and also through the back of his knees. There was a lot of blood loss, I think he might have been on warfarin or some other type of blood thinner, I'll need to check his medical records for that." Ellie nodded and then turned to face the violent scene before her, she needed to study it as she worked Cottons case more than anyone, she wanted to see just how close this copycat was to the original.

The scene looked like a grotesque gothic sculpture, blood had dried down this man's arms and legs. The grass around the tree was trampled and his shoes, which were lying a few feet away, were scuffed and muddy. He struggled before being impaled, so the victim was conscious and alert, the same as Cotton's M.O. Ellie got close to examine the nails struck through his knees, they had been painted blood red, another thing Cotton always did but also wasn't reported. She stood up and turned to leave. "You'll let me know what you find?" she asked the Doc as she opened the tent.

"You're first on my speed dial I promise"

Ellie left the tent, surprised to find Gavin already outside. 'When did he leave?' she thought to herself as she walked over to him as he chatted with a young PC.

"Ah boss good, I've just been given the evidence bag of the contents of the victims pockets." Gavin handed her the plastic bag and she studied the contents, in particular the tarot card resting at the bottom of the bag. She flipped the bag over to see the reverse of the card and was not surprised to find a biblical verse written neatly on the back. Ellie took a picture of the quote on her phone and then handed the evidence bag back to the officer with instructions to get all of this over to forensics and get them to do a handwriting analysis on it. The PC nodded and left as Ellie turned back towards her car and Gavin jogged to catch her up.

"Els what the hell is this? I mean this guy has studied Cotton down to the last detail! The card, the scripture, even the bloody painted nails for Christ sake! Who could possibly have known the exact position of where he puts those nails? The knees are not common in religious depictions are they?"

"No they're not, but they make the most sense if your plan is to keep the victim upright. I agree that only someone who spent an awful lot of time discussing this with Cotton could pull this off with such detail. There is only one difference, Doc thinks the victim died of shock from blood loss."

"So he wasn't strangled?" Gavin asked confused.

"Not that she can tell, but that could have been accidental, the victim died before he got a chance to strangle them. That will frustrate him if he's going to all this trouble to imitate Cotton. I think he'll try again to get it right…we're going to have to trawl through Cotton's life since he went to prison to see who could have done this.

Chapter 5

Kate wandered into the living room and slumped on the couch, she had just finished a long zoom meeting with her publisher and sitting in the same position for so long had made her stiff.

"I feel like an old woman" she muttered to Bella and Bruiser who were dozing on the other side of the couch. The peace was disturbed by Peggy bursting through the door, she was red faced and flustered. Kate sat up alarmed at Peggy's uncharacteristic loss of cool.

"Peggy what's wrong?" she cried as Peggy sat in the chair opposite her, she started fanning herself with a newspaper like a Victorian matriarch.

"Oh Katie, your mum has a .....fancy man!" Peggy said the last part as if it was a dreadful family dishonour.

"What? Mum's got a man?" Kate asked surprised and a little amused by the look of indignation on Peggy's face.

"Aye, I got the info from a reliable source."

"What source?"

"Freida from the paper shop." Peggy said as if the name alone settled the matter. Kate started to laugh.

"Freida? Honestly Peggy, everyone knows what an old gossip that woman is!"

"True, but she's a proper gossip, takes it very seriously so wouldn't pass on something she didn't think was true."

"Right fine, so what did St Freida of the gossiping sisters have to say for herself?" Kate asked rolling her eyes.

"She saw him, you know how the paper shop is on the other side of the road from your mums house. Well Freida was serving and happened to look out to see a tall silver fox standing at our Aggie's door and then she pulled him inside quickly and slammed the door." Peggy finished by stretching out her arms in a 'see I told you' manner.

"Ach Peggy he could be in reading the gas meter for all Freida knows! That's hardly evidence is it?" Kate said in a soothing tone but Peggy wasn't listening.

"I wonder where she met him? I mean we usually go to the pub together, and the bingo...I need to do a bit of investigating..."

"Peggy don't you dare do a security check on this man, if there's something to tell then mum will tell us in her own time."

"Nuts to that, I want to know. I've got Freida on lookout for when he comes back and she's to phone me when she sees him."

"And then what? Rack or thumb screws?" Kate asked.

"How's young Ellie?" Peggy asked, clearly wanting the subject changed.

"I don't know actually, I've not heard from her today. She must be in the middle of something and can't call. She seemed fine this morning though, news that this Cotton bloke was dead seemed to calm her down. Oh by the way Bill and Ann are coming back in a couple of days, do you want to go bowling or something? A bit of family time and all that?"

"Sounds great Katie, I'll organise the troops and make the lane booking...maybe your mum's fancy man could come..."

"Peggy!" Kate warned.

"Spoilsport" she muttered as she got up to make tea.

Chapter 6

The team have gathered back at the office, all looking tired and harassed, it had been a stressful morning.

"I take it that you've all seen the throng of journos outside the main reception?" Ellie asked as the team groaned back at her.

"They've been calling all morning for quotes boss, they've been a nightmare." moaned Harris.

"I'll get the Press Office to handle them but for now, 'no comments' all round ok?" they nodded in understanding.

"What have we got on Cotton so far?"

"Well boss, Barlinnie confirmed that Cotton never shared a cell during his whole time there, he was part of a lifers unit and part of that was a guaranteed single cell on a separate landing on the wing." Harris explained as he read his notes.

"Very cushy" growled Gavin.

"So no cellmate, any friends in there that he would have imparted his murderous wisdom to?" Ellie asked.

"Nah boss, I spoke to the POs from his wing and, off the record, he was not popular among the general prison population. His sermons that he would scream into the late hours of the morning didn't win him any popularity contests and actually got him a few hidings from the young bloods in there." Harris said.

"No cell mate and no friends…brilliant…" Ellie groaned as she rubbed her face with her hands. "Visitors?"

"Ah yes boss, he's had several regular visitors over the years, his aunt came once a week and several friends, they're sending me the visitors log details this afternoon." Harris said, glad to finally have something positive to give Ellie.

"I wonder who these friends are?" pondered Kent. "I've been digging into his past, previous employers and stuff. He doesn't seem to have made friends at work but I've got a meeting with his last employer before his arrest, I'm going to see what they can tell me about him."

"Good work both of you, Gavin can you go through the victim details?" Ellie asked as she got up to put scene photos on the board.

"Ok the victim found this morning is David Matlock, aged 53, married with two grown up children. He was a District Manager at a local bookies firm, family liaison are already in place with the family boss." Gavin said as he wrote these details on the board.

"He worked for a bookies? That might explain the Bible verse written on the tarot card." Ellie muttered as she put a picture of the card up. "1 Timothy 6:9" Ellie said to the team. I looked it up and this is what it says… 'But those who desire to be rich fall into temptation, into a snare, into many senseless and harmful desires that plunge people into ruin and destruction.'" When Ellie looked up, the team were looking a bit confused. "Do you think that might be some sort of anti-gambling message in context?" Ellie asked.

"Aye, bloody hell you're right!" Gavin said in awe. "So he must have known enough about the victim to know where he worked."

"Exactly, so this isn't a random attack, David Matlock was chosen, possibly because of the gambling thing but maybe for some other reason. Have we got any forensics yet?" Ellie asked.

"Not yet Els, the Doc hasn't finished with him yet but I've been assured we will get what they have soon. What we do have though is Cotton's medical history sent over from the medical wing of the prison. What they've told us is that he suffered a heart attack in the medical wing, an ambulance was called and he was taken to the Royal Infirmary but he died in the ambulance on the way." Gavin said as he read from the report.

"Interesting, I don't remember anything about a history of heart trouble from Cotton's file." Ellie said confused.

"He doesn't have one that's why. Not a thing about his heart anywhere until two days before he died, they say he took a funny turn and was sent to the medical wing."

"Huh...interesting..." Ellie commented but then turned back to the board to study the scene pictures once more.

Chapter 7

Kate crossed the road as quickly as she could, avoiding the late afternoon traffic and got into the passenger seat of the car parked behind a delivery van. When she sat down she sighed as she looked out the window.

"Peggy please tell me that you didn't call me down here on the pretext of an emergency just to sit in a borrowed car to stake out mum's house!" she said in frustration. Peggy didn't respond right away as she had mini binoculars attached to her face.

"Peggy!" Kate bellowed and Peggy dropped the binoculars.

"Katie there's no need to shout, I'm an old woman, you could have given me a turn" she said clutching her chest.

"Bollocks, you're healthier than me and you know it. What are we doing here?"

"Freida called me, he's in there Katie, in there with your mum right now!"

"So?" Kate really didn't see the problem here.

"She's drawn the curtains! In the living room!" Peggy blurted this out as if Aggie was running a disorderly house.

"Peggy it's none of our business what's going on in there, let's go before she spots us, god knows how we would explain what we're doing here." Kate said as she started to get out of the car.

"Ach she won't spot us, it's not my car, as far as she knows it's just an average person's car." Peggy shrugged.

"Peggy it's a powder blue audi with eyelashes painted on the headlights! This thing would stand out even being driven through a Pride march! Where did you get it from anyway?"

"It's one of the analyst lassies at work, she's um… quirky with her taste." Peggy said. "Oh look out, the door's opening!" Peggy slid lower in her seat and Kate followed. They watched as a tall, tanned, handsome silver haired man stepped out of Aggie's front door followed by a sweating and exhausted looking Aggie. They watched as Aggie handed over a wad of banknotes to him, he kissed her cheek and walked off in the direction of the subway. Peggy clutched Kate's arm in horror "Oh God…her fancy man is a gigolo!"

Chapter 8

Ellie got home and kicked off her shoes, glad to be home after a long day. She made her way through to the living room and was given the usual waggy bum greeting from Bruiser and an aging Bella got up a bit slower to greet her. Ellie bent down to give both a hello and after the two had given her welcome kisses, they went back to sleeping on the couch. She followed the voices into the kitchen to find Kate and Peggy drinking tea at the kitchen table looking pale.

"What's wrong with you two?" Ellie asked as she kissed Kate hello and gave Peggy's shoulder a squeeze as she went to the teapot to make herself a cup.

"Peggy's traumatised." Kate responded as she rolled her eyes.

"What happened?"

"I'll tell you what's happened, my only sister, Katie's mother is…cavorting with some paid fancy man! Oh the shame of it!"

"Oh come on!" said Ellie laughing "on what planet does Aggie pay a male sex worker?"

"We've seen him Ellie!" sniffed Peggy "he was coming out of her house this afternoon and she gave him money on the doorstep."

"There will be a logical explanation Peggy." Ellie said reasonably but amused at the thought of her mother in law and a gigolo.

"I'm telling you this, I'll get to the bottom of it, I'm not having her dragging the family name through the mud!"

"Family name? Where are we Downton? Who's going to find out even if it is true?" Kate said impatiently.

"Freida will talk! All the neighbours going in for the papers, she won't be able to contain herself… gossiping old cow."

"As if anyone is going to believe Freida? You forget she's still in the bad books with the neighbours for that pyramid scheme fiasco last year." Kate said, trying to stop Peggy doing something stupid. She turned back to Ellie with her eyes wide "How was work honey?" an obvious change of subject and Ellie smiled but went along with it.

"Not great if I'm honest, we got a body this morning, murder victim and the way he was killed is identical to how Cotton killed his victims." Ellie said as Kate squeezed her hand.

"But it can't be Cotton, he's dead right?" Peggy asked.

"Yeah he's dead so we're working on the theory that it's a copycat but this guy must have had a lot of contact with Cotton to get the details right, he couldn't have done this just by reading about the murders in the press."

"What are you planning to do to catch him?" asked Kate.

"We catch him through Cotton, we work through who had access to Cotton and eliminate them as we go. There can't be that many people who were close enough to him." Ellie said with confidence and a smile but inside she didn't feel the confidence she displayed, there was a fear gnawing at her and she couldn't explain why. Her musings were interrupted by the arrival of Aggie looking tired as she dropped shopping bags in the kitchen.

"Aggie dear you look knackered! What on earth have you been up to?" Peggy asked innocently as Kate rolled her eyes and Ellie supressed a grin.

"Oh just the house work, dusting and such but it's wiped me out. I must be getting old." she said as she unpacked the shopping.

"You're definitely getting something" Peggy muttered under her breath and Ellie choked on the tea she had just drank. Thankfully Aggie missed this exchange and carried on fussing over the shopping. Kate took pity on her mum. "Why don't we order something in, you do look tired mum." She said with feeling.

"Aye, that would be nice, I could do with a sit down and a cuppa. But none of that sushi you made us try last time, I had the runs for days!" Aggie complained.

Ellie sat back and relaxed a bit as she watched the family argue over what to order, this normality was just what she needed as she was more worried than she would have admitted about this new evil lurking over Glasgow.

Chapter 9

Ellie had slept in this morning, she had been conned into a poker game with Peggy that lasted until the early hours when Aggie came thundering into the kitchen in her rollers and fluffy slippers and read the riot act to both of them and sent them to their beds. Ellie was relieved as she was at least £50 down by then. She arrived a little late into the office and the team was already gathered for the briefing as she hugged her coffee cup to her like it was the last life vest on the Titanic.

"Are we all ready?" Ellie asked. "Where's Harris?" she noticed his seat was empty. Then she heard some groans and a giggle.

"He had a hot date last night boss" Gavin explained.

"He's been banging on about this new bloke for a couple of days now." Kent said as she rolled her eyes.

"Gentleman callers seem to be all the rage" Ellie muttered to herself. "So what have we got kids?"

she said louder to bring the briefing to order.

"Well David Matlock was covering a managers shift at the bookies on Hope Street." Gavin began reading from his notes. "We spoke to the staff that were on shift with him, they said he closed the shop at 9pm and had a smoke with one of the girls until her taxi showed up and then he walked away towards Buchanan Street Subway Station. We've sent uniform down to get the CCTV from the station to see if he reaches it."

"That's a priority, we need to know when and where he met his killer, he wouldn't have had a reason to be in that graveyard at night unless he was local maybe?" Ellie thought out loud.

"I checked that Ma'am, he lives just off Great Western Road and normally gets the subway to Kelvinbridge station when he's working. No reason for him to be near the graveyard." Kent said from her seat.

"Ok, forensics?" Ellie asked.

"They've pulled DNA off the victim and the scene but haven't got any hits yet." Kent replied.

"Ok our focus today is follow the victim, I want to know his every move from 9pm when he left work. Kent I want you to get on to the Necropolis staff and see if you can get the CCTV from the cameras at the main gate. I want to know if Matlock walked through those gates of his own volition or if he was driven there." Kent nodded her understanding and then went to answer her phone as Ellie divided up investigative roles.

"Ma'am, we've got another body, it's in the same graveyard. No ID as yet, found by a dog walker this morning." Kent said hurriedly.

"Tell them we're on our way." Ellie said as she got up "Oh and when Harris finally drags his hungover arse into work, tell him from me that he owes everyone a coffee for being a dirty stop out!" she quipped.

"Yeah" chimed Gavin "and also tell him that I want to know *Ev-ery-thing!*"

Chapter 10

Kate was walking back from the park after a long walk to try to burn off some of Bruisers energy. This culminated in her trying to bribe him out of the duck pond with a promise of a treat.

"Look at you acting like butter wouldn't melt" she grumbled to him as he gave her a lopsided doggy grin around his favourite ball. He had twigs stuck to his face and mud from the neck down. Bella gave him a disapproving look as she walked daintily beside Kate, not a speck of mud on her white fur. As Kate turned the corner onto her street she spotted a marked police car sitting outside her house. Panic gripped her. "Oh no, Ellie" she gasped. She ran down the road towards the car and almost collapsed when she got to it and she found Peggy sat in the back looking sheepish.

"Peggy? What the f…"

PC Simpson got out of the car and smiled at Kate, recognising her from all the business with Val. She winked as she raised her voice so that Peggy could hear from inside the car.

"Is this one yours ma'am?" PC Simpson said as she stuck her thumb in Peggy's direction. Kate could read Peggy's lips as she mouthed 'this one?!'

"Yes PC Simpson I'm afraid this is another one of my relatives that I need to apologise for. What's she done?" Kate asked as she gave Peggy the death stare that would have made Aggie proud.

"We got a call about a person behaving suspiciously at a paper shop in Bearsden. We arrived to find this lady stood in an out of order phone box with binoculars."

Kate groaned "Of course she was. Look..." Kate spoke quietly at this point "my mum, her sister possibly has a new man friend and for some reason she's acting like a mad woman over this. I'm really sorry about all this." She said earnestly.

"Don't worry about it, my old dad was just the same sometimes, the calls I used to get about him! Anyway, I've not charged her but thought it best to bring her here to keep her out of trouble." PC Simpson replied with a smile.

"Trouble, I'll give her trouble" Kate muttered as she opened the car door and Peggy got out with as much dignity as she could muster.

"Get in the house you old reprobate."

Kate said her goodbyes to PC Simpson as Peggy took the dogs inside. When Kate got in she had done some calming breathing so that she didn't choke Peggy with a dog lead.

"What the *hell* did you think you were playing at?!" roared Kate, the breathing exercises a complete failure. The dogs scarpered to safety quicker than they've moved in years as Peggy sat like a school kid in front of the headmaster.

"I want to know why she's lying to me" Peggy said quietly.

"Peggy did it ever occur to you that she's not lying, but wants to see where this is going before subjecting the poor bloke to us lot?" Kate said exasperated. Peggy shrugged in a non-comital fashion.

"Enough now Peggy, you're behaving like a lunatic. Now hand me over your kit bag".

"What kit bag?" Peggy said evasively.

"You know bloody well what kit bag! Your surveillance bag, the one I used to help you pack when I was little before mum caught me playing with a ninja star." Kate clicked her fingers to spur Peggy into action. She got up and pulled the bag from under her bulky coat and handed it to Kate.

"Thank you, you won't be needing your binoculars any more, nor will you need …" Kate started to rummage through the bag. "Your night vision goggles….what were you planning on doing with those?!" Kate kept pulling stuff out of the bag as

Peggy watched. "A taser?! A bloody taser?! Why not drag the Royal Artillery and some tanks in to complete the set! Just wait until Ellie hears about this!" Kate warned Peggy as she marched her into the kitchen with her bag of tricks.

Chapter 11

Gavin and Ellie return once again to the Necropolis, this time using the entrance at the opposite side of this vast city of the dead. They turn off Balmore Road and pass through the stone archway of the gates and follow the road to the left until they reach the taped cordon. The weather is gloomy this morning and the wind whipped through the trees as they stepped out of the car and walked through a gap in the trees into the more open expanse of the graveyard. This area was different to the bit they were at yesterday, the headstones and monuments were more ornate and religious in style. They walked past several large depictions of Jesus and Mary depicted in marble as part of the final resting place of several Italian families.

"Quite eerie this" muttered Gavin as he shivered a little. He had a fear of statues that normally kept him out of graveyards and memorial places. He gave an angel statue a particularly wide berth as he walked behind Ellie.

"Really?" she asked exasperated.

"Shut up, if you ever watched Doctor Who you would be scared of these too!" he complained. "If that thing moves I'm out of here and you are on your own!" he declared as they continued walking towards the forensic tent at the end of the path. Doctor Brett was standing outside of the tent, her mask in her hand as she talked to a uniformed officer. When she noticed Ellie and Gavin she stopped talking and walked hurriedly towards them. Ellie could tell by her face that something was seriously wrong.

"Hey Doc, what's up?" Gavin asked but Ellie stopped as she saw that the Doc was struggling for composure, her eyes red like she had been crying recently.

"Ellie...don't go in there just now...there's something we need to talk about." Doc said gently as she steered both Ellie and Gavin towards the treeline for privacy.

"Doc what is it? Tell me!" Ellie was alarmed at her friend's distress. Then it dawned on her "Who is it Doc?"

"I'm so sorry Ellie...I didn't know until I got here and saw the body...by then you were already on your way and I didn't know what to do..." she babbled.

"Who is it Doc?" Ellie asked once more.

"I'm sorry...it's Harris." Doc replied, tears filling her eyes once more.

Gavin lurched back and sat down on a tree stump, pale and shocked. He had always been fond of young Harris and was very protective of him. Ellie just stood still taking this information in. She used all of her inner strength to keep herself contained in the moment, she needed to remain clinical. Harris needed her to be at her best. This thought caught her and pierced her heart, she took a few deep breaths and willed the tears forming to recede. She placed her grief, shock and anger into a box and steadied herself. She looked into the sympathetic eyes of Doctor Brett and asked "What happened to him?"

"Oh Ellie...you know what happened to him." Doc started but she saw that Ellie needed something to focus on so she carried on. "He's been strangled, I believe that to be cause of death..." she hesitated once more.

"How was his body left Doc?" Ellie urged.

"He...um....He's been attached to the monument on top of the grave. Jesus carrying the cross... Harris is draped over the cross." They heard a noise behind them as Gavin retched into the grass, he sat back down miserably as tears clouded his vision. "That bastard" he groaned in his agony.

"I want to see the scene Doc" Ellie said quietly.

"I don't think that's..." Doc started.

"Me too." Gavin responded, his eyes full of determined rage.

"Ok...I shouldn't let you, this is a conflict of interest and you know it. Go take a look before they take you off this case."

Ellie and Gavin entered the tent, it was quiet except for their own shaky breaths. They looked at the scene with sadness and horror.

"He's wearing his pulling clothes" Gavin said gruffly as he choked back tears. "I picked that outfit for him last year, he wanted to attract a more mature man...he's only 23 for Christ sake!"

Harris looked young in death, Ellie could see the strangulation marks around his pale neck. He had been tied to the monument by a length of rope and Ellie noticed with a pang that nails had been driven through his knees and hands. They could stand it no longer and left the tent hurriedly. Doc Brett was standing outside, her face lined in misery.

"Doc I want everything you can give me on this, I want forensics to drop whatever they are doing...this is now their priority" Ellie stated with determination. "I'll need to go tell his mum..."Ellie said quietly.

"No...let me do it Els...his mum was my teacher at school...I know the family well. Could you tell the team? I don't think I could face it..." Gavin admitted.

"I will...we'll get this bastard Gav...I swear it!"

Chapter 12

Back at the office Ellie stood outside the office door watching, Kent was bustling around making coffee and laughing at a joke someone must have said to her. Ellie really didn't know how she was going to tell her, Kent came through the academy with Harris, they had been friends for years. Steeling herself, she took a deep breath and walked in quietly.

"Ah boss you're just in time, I'm making coffee. Harris still hasn't arrived in so it must have been a hell of a night" Kent said cheerfully as she spooned copious amounts of sugar into her own coffee. Her good natured expression disappeared when she looked at Ellie properly and saw her red eyes and heartbroken expression.

"What's happened?"

"I'm…the body found this morning…it was Harris. He's been killed by this copycat killer. I'm so sorry." Ellie said as she choked back the tears she was desperately holding back. Kent sat for a moment in shock, tears silently falling into her lap. She looked back up, pain and anger flashing through eyes but also determination.

"Are you sure it was this killer?"

"We are sure yes, same M.O." Ellie said, sparing Kent the details.

"So we catch this bastard then" growled Kent as she pushed herself up from the chair and walked towards the board to look through what they already know.

"Kent...if you need time..." Ellie began but Kent shook her head.

"No, I need to work, need to keep my focus...oh what about his mum!" Kent said in a panic.

"Gav has gone to see her, he knows her and the family." Ellie explained, a little bit put out that she didn't know this fact until today. She thought she knew her team well, maybe she didn't.

"So do we know the name of this bloke he was meeting last night?" Ellie asked, hoping that focusing on work was indeed what Kent needed right now.

"He never mentioned his name, just called him 'my new man' all the time." Kent said as she scrolled through her phone. "His Instagram had him at Ashton Lane last night and then no new posts after that. Harris was never off his social media so that in itself is unusual." Kent said as she continued scrolling. "Did you find his phone Ma'am?"

"Yes, I think it's with forensics right now, why?"

"You should check his dating apps, that's where he met most of his dates from and I'm sure that's where he met this guy too."

"His dating apps? Ok, that's next on the list I'll text Gav and see if he can swing by to pick it up on his way in." Ellie said thinking aloud as she sent a quick message to Gavin. She got an instant response back from him.

<Great minds Els, I've just stopped by to pick up his phone. His dad said to look at it. Be there in a few.>

"Gav has the phone and is coming round now. Harris was working on the visitor list before he left yesterday...we should see what he found on that and continue to go through it. Are you up for that?"

"Yes Ma'am" Kent said as she walked over to Harris' desk, she hesitated for a moment but took a deep breath and started to go through his files. Gavin arrived looking like he had been through the emotional wringer.

"How did the family take it?" Ellie asked him as he dropped the clear evidence bag on the table and pressed the 'on' switch through the plastic, he was concentrating on watching the phone reboot and trying to steady his own emotions.

"Bad Els...his mum needed sedation after we told

her. His dad is looking after her now but he's devastated himself. I asked him a few questions while the nurse was in with Mrs Harris. They didn't know who Harris was seeing last night, said he was so popular they couldn't keep up with him." Gavin said with a sad smile. He was interrupted by Harris' phone making a little chirp, the looked down to see a notification saying 'posted'. At almost the same time, Kent's phone pinged a notification. She opened her phone and went deathly pale, she threw her phone on the table and looked like she was ready to pass out.

"H...his gram account...h...he's just uploaded a photo..." was all they could get out of Kent before she fled to the bathroom to be sick. Ellie and Gavin ran towards her phone still lying on the desk and grabbed it. What they saw, horrified them.

"What the hell?!"

"The sick bastard must have sent this and then switched the phone off...it would only send once the phone was switched on again...how...how can it be..." Gavin trailed off as there was no logical explanation for the image they were staring at.

The killer had used Harris' phone to take a selfie of himself with Harris' body. Ellie's world was spinning, as she stared in horror at the photo.

The killer was John Cotton.

Chapter 13

"How the hell is this even possible?!" the Chief thundered as he paced up and down behind his desk. Ellie had moments before ran into his office, still holding Kent's phone, to tell him what they had found.

"Could this have been faked? My daughter is always doing things with her pictures...could that be a thing?" The Chief asked, almost in desperation, as the thought of Cotton being alive and at large was almost too much to comprehend. He stopped pacing and looked over at Ellie who hadn't moved since she arrived.

"We honestly don't know Sir, Gavin is already over at forensics with Harris' phone and the tech analyst is going to investigate it. He's also getting them to pull it off social media so that his family don't see it. The last thing we need is for this picture to go viral." Ellie explained as her heart thundered in her chest, the thought of Harris' body being used as a meme was too much for her.

"Ok…I'm owed a favour from the head of counter terrorism… I'm going to ask for a loan of their social media expert to figure out if this photo is faked." The Chief began.

"Don't waste the favour Sir…if it is fake, our analyst will be able to tell." Ellie said with confidence.

"How are you so sure?"

"Let's just say…off the record…that this particular analyst had a little extra tutelage in online forensics from someone in the security services." Ellie explained as cryptically as she could without telling him the truth that Peggy had brought her own slightly illegal hacker in to give Annie a crash course.

"Ok…I'll trust you that it's something I don't need to know. So…now for the hard question. If this photo is real…Cotton is loose…how has this happened?"

"The answer to that lies at Barlinnie I think Sir, and I think that's where we have to concentrate our investigation. It was what Harris had started to do before…well…before." Ellie finished quietly.

"Ellie…" The Chief sighed. "By rights I should be taking you and your team off this case. Your involvement could prejudice a trial. Before you jump down my throat" he began as he sensed Ellie was about to but in. "In this instance however, I'll be recommending that you stay on…no one knows

Cotton better than you and Gavin, you worked his case for months, you got in his head. We need that more than to keep the CPS happy, lives are being lost. Don't make me regret this choice Ellie, by the book." He warned her quietly as there was a sharp wrap on the door and Gavin entered.

"Sir, Ma'am, the picture has been taken down and thankfully the family didn't see it, I got family liaison to double check. Annie in forensics is working her magic right now on his phone. I... um...I had an idea and got Doc Brett to run the DNA found at the scene with some of Cotton's that I knew we still held in storage...it matched. It's him." Gavin said quietly.

"How on earth did he not flag up on the system?" asked the Chief.

"I expect that his details were removed from the active DNA database when he 'died'" Ellie said with air quotes.

"That was my hunch too...I also thought it would be the quickest way to authenticate the image." He explained.

"Excellent work Detective. I want you both on this round the clock, any resources you need, you'll get them. Just catch this evil bastard before he wreaks havoc on Glasgow." The Chief told them before dismissing them.

Chapter 14

"Hi honey, I thought you'd forgotten about us today." Kate joked as she heard the front door and the scampering of paws that announced Ellie's arrival. She walked through to the living room and knew instantly that something bad had happened. Ellie wasn't play fighting with Bruiser or chasing the dogs around, instead Kate found her sat cross-legged on the floor, Bella in her lap and Bruiser lying beside her, as if they felt her mood and wanted to comfort her. Ellie was absently scratching Bella's ear as she stared into space.

"What's wrong?" Kate asked gently as she got gingerly down on the floor beside her wife.

"It's not a copycat...Cotton's alive. He's alive and free and killing people...he...he killed Harris last night..." the last bit came out in a sob as Ellie finally broke down and cried for her friend. Kate hugged her tightly and gently rocked her to soothe her as she cried out the rage and grief that she had been holding back until she was in her safe place, with Kate.

They don't know how long they stayed cuddled on the floor but Peggy walked through the door to find them still there, even the dogs hadn't moved from their protective vigil.

"What on earth has happened?!" Peggy was alarmed to see Ellie needing comforted. "Both of you up now! You'll get piles sitting on the cold floor like that!"

She pulled the two up and led them both to the sofas. Kate kissed Ellie before getting up. "I'll go make us some tea…tell Peggy" she squeezed her hand and left them to it.

"Cotton is back, he's not dead." Ellie started. She felt Peggy stiffen beside her.

"How do you know for sure?"

"He took a selfie with his latest victim…Harris…"

"I see…and its verified?" Peggy was in work mode.

"Yes, our analyst has confirmed the metadata to be genuine and unaltered."

"Ok then…what do you need me to do? I assume that finding you slumped on the ground just then means that you are scared for the family?" Peggy said this bluntly but not unkindly and squeezed Ellie's hand in a gruff reassurance.

"I need you all not to be alone, don't go anywhere alone…I don't trust that Cotton won't try to come for either me or my loved ones." Ellie said quietly.

"Ok then, you leave that with me young Ellie and I'll make sure that none of us leave this house alone. I'll get Aggie to come stay and we will make this a fortress. I've got a few people that owe me some favours for, let's just say the disappearance of some embarrassing documents. I'll make sure that we are secure. You deal with catching this man."

Kate walked in with the tea and looked to both to see what the plan was.

"So what have we to do honey?" Kate asked as she handed a cup of tea over.

"Don't go anywhere alone basically, Peggy has agreed to move in for the duration and she's going to go get Aggie to do the same. I'm sorry that, once again I'm bringing danger to our family...." Ellie began but Kate interrupted her.

"Stop that right now, you aren't the cause of this, he is. Besides, I've grown up with this old reprobate as an aunt. I've never told you about the time I was kidnapped by a Moroccan arms cartel when I was 9 did I?" Kate said with a smile.

"Oh stop being so melodramatic, you weren't kidnapped! They borrowed you for a bit, you were perfectly safe." Scoffed Peggy. "Besides Farouq brought you a lovely teddy bear over with him."

"It was filled with cash to give to some bloke in Customs!" Kate argued. "And if I was just 'borrowed'" she said using air quotes "then why were you banned from seeing me for 6 months?"

Kate asked with her eyebrow raised.

"Well...I mean...your mother was just being a helicopter parent about the whole thing. You had a nice day out and got to meet some lovely new people, forgive me for trying to bring culture to your life" muttered Peggy as she got up to grab a biscuit from the tray.

"What the hell did I marry in to?" muttered Ellie as she sat clutching her tea listening to the madness that was her extended family.

"Enough reminiscing, I'll call our Aggie and get her to come over. I really don't trust this fancy man of hers...what if he's in league with this Cotton character? I need to keep her safe" Peggy said with sadness and it was then that Kate finally realised that Peggy wasn't jealous of her mum, she was scared for her. She had already had one abusive relationship and Kate knew that Peggy blamed herself for not protecting her.

"Peggy talk to mum, tell her how you feel, I'm sure this man is perfectly normal and you're worrying over nothing."

"Ellie do you have a photo of this Cotton man?" asked Peggy. Ellie scrolled through her phone to find the screenshot of the image from Harris' phone.

"It's the most up to date image we have...it's not a pleasant picture though."

Peggy looked at it and seemed to relax a little. "He doesn't look like the man that was at Aggies."

"I wouldn't have thought so, from what Kate tells me, he's quite the dishy sort"

"If you like that sort of thing…" grumbled Peggy.

"Cotton isn't, he's a potbellied, long haired, greasy weirdo. Aggie wouldn't go near him." Ellie said and Peggy seemed to relax at her words.

"Get Aggie over here and explain the situation to her, try not to terrify her though Peggy" warned Ellie as Peggy gave her a 'who me?' look.

"What are you going to be doing?" Kate asked.

"I need to go over to Barlinnie and figure out how the hell Cotton managed to pull this off".

Chapter 15

HMP Barlinnie was the epitome of an old Victorian prison. It loomed large over the area looking like a Dickensian work house. Only the main entrance had been updated but the wings were still draughty and outdated. It housed the majority of Scotland's most violent criminals but was planned for demolishment to make way for a new super-prison. Ellie personally thought that just looking at Barlinnie would be enough to scare most people from ever doing wrong.

Ellie and Gavin were escorted through the main admin block of the prison to meet the prison Governor Phil Hastings. They were shown into his plush office, the thick carpet masking their footsteps.

"Ah Detective Superintendent, good to see you, have you been offered coffee?" Phil Hastings started, all smiles and politeness. Ellie knew these were the actions of a man who knew his staff had fucked up somewhere. They sat down and faced him as he shuffled some paperwork on his desk.

"Mr Hastings..." Ellie began.

"Oh Phil please I insist" he smarmed.

"Phil, can you give us a rundown of the events of the night that Cotton escaped this prison?" Ellie wasn't messy about, she needed answers.

"Well...ahem...obviously I am conducting a stringent investigation into this matter...but I'll tell you what I've been told so far. After dinner, Cotton went to his cell saying he felt unwell. The wing nurse came to see him and gave him two paracetamol for the pain he said he was feeling. A few hours later, just before lockup, he was found collapsed in his landing. He was immediately taken to the medical wing for assessment and he was monitored through the night by the shift Doctor and nursing staff."

"And this was the night before his escape?" Gavin interjected and Phil nodded.

"Yes...now where was I? Oh yes, he remained in the medical wing the next day and according to the medical notes that I have here, he took a downturn in the evening and his heart stopped. Medical staff worked on him as an ambulance was called. The ambulance arrived within minutes and the paramedics took over, getting him stable enough to move him to the Royal Infirmary with a Prison Officer as escort. We were informed shortly after that Cotton had died in the ambulance on the way."

"We need the names of the medical staff who looked after him and the officer that went in the ambulance with him." Ellie said.

"Of course, according to the notes there was a Doctor and three nursing staff on shift that night, I'll get my secretary to get their contact details for you."

"Thank you, I wonder though…what happened to his body?" Ellie asked as she made notes.

"Well we were told that he was sent straight to the city morgue, his family refused to claim the body so he was cremated and his remains scattered by crematorium staff." Phil said with a shrug.

"His family didn't claim him?" Ellie was confused. "His aunt visited him every week without fail, protested his innocence to anyone that would listen. You're telling me that she didn't want to claim his body for burial?"

"All I can tell you is that the family were contacted and they refused to claim the body. Maybe she had a change of heart in the end?" Phil responded.

"Thank you for your time, we may need to come back to interview your staff, I trust we have your full cooperation in this matter?"

"Oh of course, whatever you need." Phil said nervously.

Outside the prison Ellie was thinking hard.

"What's going on in that noggin Els?" Gavin asked as they picked their way through the car park.

"Cotton's aunt loved him…like the Kray twins mother loved them. There is no way in hell that she leaves her sainted nephew to be cremated alone. I think that he wasn't claimed so that he could be cremated quickly and scattered so that the body couldn't be checked." Ellie said.

"So you think his aunt knew he wasn't dead." Gavin asked.

"I do, I think he needed a lot of help to pull this off both inside and outside the prison. We need to figure out who had the ability or the inclination to help him."

"Tomorrows plan then is to track down all the staff and Cottons friends?" Gavin asked with a yawn as they got into the car.

"Yup, that's the plan. Gav…um…I don't want to seem like an alarmist…but is your family safe?" Ellie had been worried about Gavin and his young brood since she realised that they could be targets.

"Don't worry Els, I've sent Mhairi and the kids up to her parents' house. Her dad is ex SAS so will keep them safe, besides I'm pretty sure Mhairi could take Cotton if she thought the kids were in danger, she has a hell of a left hook. So do you mind if I move into Apocalypse Mansion with you? I promise I'll tidy up after myself!" he said jokingly.

"Of course, I was going to offer anyway, although it means spending your evenings with Aggie and Peggy." Ellie joked back. Gavin looked horrified.

"Please tell me that you've locked up the wine".

"As if a padlock would stop those two." laughed Ellie as they started the long drive home.

Chapter 16

Ellie and Gavin got home to find the clan all assembled in the living room. Bella and Bruiser bypassed Ellie entirely to jump on Gavin who got down on his hands and knees and started to play with the pups.

"Traitors" muttered Ellie as she walked into the living room and sat down next to Kate. Aggie was furiously messaging on her phone, a little smile on her lips as Peggy watched her like a hawk.

"You cheating on me Aggie?" quipped Gavin as he sat down, jolting her to nervously stash her phone back in her pocket. "No son, you're still my favourite." Aggie recovered her composure in time to reply as she gave him a squeeze.

"Right, family meeting" bellowed Peggy so loudly that everyone jumped and Bella growled.

"Calm down for God sake Peggy, our nerves are frazzled as it is!" Kate ordered as she massaged her leg that she knocked against the table in fright.

"Sorry dears, but this is serious. Eleanor what are

we facing here?"

"Eleanor?" Kate mouthed as Ellie shrugged.

"Ok, I've already explained what Cotton did when we met last time." She rubbed at the scar on her hand absently. "We know for sure that Cotton is currently out of prison and back to his murderous ways. We know this because of the picture that I showed you Peggy, and a DNA match found at the latest crime scene. We know now, after our visit to Barlinnie this evening that he had to have had help inside the prison and outside, in order to pull this off."

"How did he get out?" asked Kate, her criminal mind clicking in.

"He was sent to the medical wing where his heart stopped and then an ambulance was sent for, he died on the way to the hospital." Ellie replied.

"Except he didn't die. Can you get his body?" asked Aggie.

"No, he was cremated almost immediately as his body was refused by his family." Ellie explained.

"You think the family are in on it, cremated so that there's no body to find?" Kate asked and Ellie nodded.

"So the help he would have needed, I presume you're thinking about the medical staff?"

"Yes, and possibly the paramedics and his prison escort, I mean they were the ones that pronounced him." Ellie said.

"But...how could they pronounce him honey? Legally a Doctor needs to do that or else no death certificate. So how did they do that?" Kate asked. Ellie hadn't thought of that bit. She was right.

"We need to interview everyone who had contact with him over those two days. We need a timeline and we need to investigate every step of what happened." Ellie said to Gavin and he nodded as he started sending texts to the team about what to do the next morning.

"Can we help?" Kate asked.

"You already have, I hadn't thought about the paramedics role properly and now I need to talk to them urgently. You could help by using that brain of yours to figure out how Cotton could fake his heart stopping".

Ellie looked around at her little family and sighed. "I'm sorry that you all have to be here and that your lives have been put on hold. I promise I'll do everything I can to catch him so that he doesn't hurt us anymore."

"Oh Ellie stop blaming yourself, we can treat this like a giant slumber party! Now where is the key to the wine cellar?" Aggie asked excitedly as Gavin groaned beside her.

Chapter 17

When Ellie and Gavin arrived at the office, Kent was already there. In fact Ellie didn't think she had been home. She looked tired but determined.

"Kent have you been here all night?" Ellie asked.

"Yes Ma'am, I...um...didn't really feel like going home, my boyfriend is away on a stag do to the Algarve so I would have been home alone." Kent said with embarrassment.

"Why didn't you say something? We have plenty of room if you want to stay with us? Gavin has already moved in for the duration so you would be more than welcome."

"Thank you Ma'am but if it's all the same to you, I'd rather just camp down here, I think better at night so I can work undisturbed here."

"Don't blame you Kent, you missed a late night rendition of 'Dancing Queen' that only ended when Peggy tried to do the splits and nearly suffocated Bruiser." Gavin warned and Kent stifled a giggle.

"The offer is open anyway Kent. Just let me know." Ellie said as she kicked Gavin.

"To business! Kent I want you to go to the ambulance station and track down the paramedics that took the 999 call to Barlinnie. I want their details and then we can interview them later. Gavin we will split this list of medical staff between us and go see each of them, hopefully they are on shift to make it easier. We also need someone here to coordinate the data and do background checks on the staff and visitors, I've requested PC Simpson from Maryhill to be seconded over to help us for this case and she will be here this afternoon. Kent if you're back by then, show her the ropes and what we need from her. She's quick so she should be able to hit the ground running." Ellie said as she then stopped and looked down before continuing with the next bit. "There is to be a memorial for Harris, the Chief is arranging it and will give us the details...but until then, there's a bucket been put in the break room, the entire station have been contributing already... it's for Harris' family, to help with the funeral and whatever else they may need. That's all...let's get to work."

Chapter 18

Gavin and Ellie return to Barlinnie to meet with the medical staff that they were informed were working today. Ellie went to talk to the on staff Doctor, Dr McKillop. It was obvious that words had been had and that he was here under duress, no doubt from Governor Phil. Dr McKillop was the very model of what an old school GP looked like. He was wearing a white coat (they don't wear those nowadays) he was thinning on top and looked like he enjoyed many a good lunch. Close to retirement he looked arrogant and bored. Ellie introduced herself and he barely looked up from his desk and merely grunted and pointed at a seat opposite him.

"Doctor I'm here to investigate exactly what occurred on the night that Cotton escaped from this ward. Can you tell me what happened in your own words?"

"My dear girl, if I used my own words I would lose you completely, you would need years of medical training to keep up. I'll keep it simple for you." He began.

'The audacity of this guy' thought Ellie as she controlled her temper and kept her facial expressions to polite interest.

"He had a heart attack, plain and simple. I don't see why everyone is making such a fuss, he's no loss." He muttered.

"We're making a fuss because he's not dead Doctor. Did he have a history of heart trouble?"

"Well no but you just had to look at him, overweight, middle aged, took no exercise… walking time bomb." He responded as if it was the most simple of things. Ellie thought he should look in the mirror when he was discussing walking time bombs but she carried on.

"Doctor why did you automatically assume heart attack when the man had no history of heart trouble…" he interrupted her here.

"Look young woman, I've been doing this since before you were born! I've worked here long enough to see what it's like, this place is full of malingerers and con artists."

"How did you treat Cotton?" she interrupted his rant.

"I told the nurse to give him two paracetamol, he was just looking for a comfy bed and good grub."

"If you thought that, why do you now say heart attack?"

"Well…he might have started off lying his way in

here but it's obvious something killed him didn't it, it's always the heart." He said arrogantly and Ellie wanted to slap him. He was contradicting himself because he didn't actually look at Cotton, he assumed and ignored. She knew that purely on his behaviour. God help anyone who was genuinely ill in this place.

"Did you call the ambulance for him?" Ellie asked coldly.

"I did not, one of the nurses must have done it in a panic. I would have just left it to fate personally." He said dismissively.

"Can you tell me which prison officer went as his escort?" Ellie hadn't been given that detail by Governor.

"Oh how should I know, all these young men look the same in that uniform."

Ellie left him to his paperwork, determined to get him investigated by the Medical Council as quickly as possible.

Ellie made her way over to Gavin who was talking to a nurse and had motioned for her to join him.

"Ah boss this is Marlene, Marlene could you tell Detective Superintendent McVey what you've just told me?" he asked kindly. Marlene nodded, she looked exhausted but good natured.

"Aye son, it was a funny night right enough. First off, the usual night shift nurse Sandra called in sick, she had it coming out at both ends she said. Food poisoning she said but not to worry, she'd sorted a bank nurse to come in and fill."

"Did Sandra miss her shift often?" asked Ellie.

"Naw, Sandra was never sick a day in her life, that's what was so funny. She had the constitution of an ox, I'd watched her eat out of date scotch pies by the dozen and never get sick. Anyway this wee lassie shows up for the shift, Keira she said her name was. Nice enough wee lassie, she even volunteered to look after that Cotton one which suited me, gave me the creeps that one, I don't trust fake God botherers."

"So what happened then?" Ellie asked.

"Well I had just sat down for my tea, I'm not as young as I used to be any my ankles swell up these days, all water, I'm on tablets for it. But I was sat down and then wee Keira ran in and used the office phone to call for an ambulance, said he had stopped breathing. So I go over, that Dr McKillop wasn't interested of course, too busy playing golf on his phone, and aye right enough Cotton wasn't breathing. We worked on him for a bit, the ambulance arrived really quickly...never heard of! When I think of the time my auld maw went arse over tit doon the stairs and had to lie there for hours before an ambulance turned up... no justice in this world. Anyway before we could even explain what was going on, the paramedics had whipped an oxygen mask on him and hauled him out of here. It was about half an hour after this that we got the call to say he was deid."

"So Dr McKillop at no point came near Cotton?" Ellie clarified.

"Naw, he's worse than useless anyway, he would have got in the way. Two bottles a day he's on." she whispered conspiratorially.

"Can you tell me which prison officer escorted him in the ambulance?"

"Actually hen…I don't think I can. It used to be that I knew them all by name, friendly bunch but since privatisation, you never see the same face twice and they use temps! It's a miracle there hasn't been riots every week with the staff shortages and turnaround."

Chapter 19

Back at the office, Kent arrived just before them and Ellie gathered the team to find out what they knew so far.

"Ma'am I've been down at the ambulance station all morning, I've been through despatch call logs and talked to the shift supervisor and anything else I could think of, no ambulance crew attended a 999 call to Barlinnie that night...in fact as best we could figure out, there was no 999 call in the first place."

"Interesting, so no call was made and no ambulance was dispatched. That makes the bank nurse Keira a priority to interview and also we need to track down this mystery prison escort and whoever the hell it was that turned up with an ambulance. Also I want a word with that nurse that called in sick, Sandra. It just seems a hell of a coincidence that the one occasion that she calls in sick, this happens. And also, who do you know that calls to arrange their own cover when they're sick? Simpson, welcome on board by the way, can you get the camera footage sent over from Barlinnie? We need faces for these people. Any joy with the CCTV at the Necropolis?"

"Thanks Ma'am, glad to help. I got the CCTV but it's not the best quality, the site supervisor said the Council only put it in to deter fly tipping in the graveyard. What you can see is a light coloured van, looks like a transit based on the shape. The registration was obscured by mud or something so no luck there but there is something written on the side of the van in small black letters but the footage is too grainy to make out what it says. This was the only vehicle to drive through the main gates at night. The only other movement through the night came from dog walkers passing through."

"Good work, see if the tech folk can clean that footage up a bit for you. Did you get the CCTV from the subway?"

"Yes Ma'am, the victim definitely got off the subway at Kelvinbridge as per his routine and headed in the direction of his home. We know he never made it that far but I've tried looking at the traffic cameras along the route and I can't find him on any of them."

"Cotton must have nabbed him almost as soon as he left the station, there's cameras all over the road." Gavin said as he studied the map.

"What if he cut through the park?" Kent asked as

she studied the map too.

"Wouldn't make sense, it would take him longer to walk through the park than to cut through these streets here." Gavin said as he pointed out the normal route.

"True, but say he was maybe meeting someone? He could have walked round the back to the park and ride area of the subway and cut through the Kelvin walkway to the park from there. Its dark there and a van wouldn't look out of place." Ellie said as she too looked at the map. "We need to consider all possibilities. He had to have picked him up around this area."

<h1 style="text-align:center">Chapter 20</h1>

Kate was scrolling through the internet with a furrowed brow, something was nagging at her about Cotton and she couldn't put her finger on it. She knew she had read something important not long ago but couldn't remember where. She was interrupted by her phone ringing with Ellies ringtone.

"Hi honey, everything ok?" she asked immediately.

"Yeah everything's fine, or as fine as it can be. First off, I miss you sweetie." Ellies voice rang through the phone and it never failed to make Kate smile.

"I miss you too honey. I think we really need a holiday." Kate joked.

"You're not kidding! But we don't tell anyone where we are going. Our lot would only tag along! I'm calling just to check in and make sure you're all ok and to let you know that Gavin and I will be a bit late back tonight as we've got to go back to Barlinnie to talk to the night shift nurse."

"Ok honey, I'll see if I can get mum or Peggy to

make up some plates for you both for when you get home."

"Thanks, you're a life saver."

"I'm good at delegating" Kate corrected her with a giggle.

"Indeed you are, see if you can delegate some coffee or tea to go with it and we'll be happy. I need to go, but if you need me, call right away ok sweetie?"

"Of course, don't worry though, we're fine here and tell Gavin that Mhairi called to say all is good up at her parents. Although her dad has taken to patrolling the garden with his hunting rifle."

"Oh god, who gave him his license back?" groaned Ellie as she remembered the occasion when Gavin's father in law lost his rifle licence as he kept threatening the local parcel delivery man with it. "I better go now sweetie, hopefully this interview won't take too long. See you tonight, I love you."

"Love you too honey." Kate replied. She walked back through to the living room to tell the others when she caught Peggy in the act of looking through Aggie's phone.

"What are you doing?!" Kate hissed as she came up to Peggy's side to see her scrolling through messages.

"What does it look like I'm doing? I'm seeing what

this bloke of hers is all about. Look at some of the messages, filth!" Peggy hissed back as she looked at Aggie's phone like it was rotting entrails. "Look at this one…'you were amazing yesterday' and then this one 'I never knew you could be so bendy' I mean what is he doing to her?"

"Peggy worry more what mum will do if she catches you with her phone. Now put it back or I swear I'll tell her what you did" Kate threatened and Peggy took a step back.

"You wouldn't grass on your own beloved auntie" Peggy looked astounded.

"Try me old woman" Kate said, her face set.

"Fine" Peggy huffed as she put Aggie's phone back on the table just before Aggie came back from the bathroom.

"Everything alright?" she asked as she noticed an atmosphere in the room.

"Yeah, Ellie called to say they would be late home. Would one of you be able to make them a plate up for later?" Kate said breezily.

"I'll do it, can't have my boy wasting away" Peggy said as she left the room quickly.

"Her boy" Aggie muttered "what about poor Ellie? I think she's losing the plot you know, she's been acting daft lately. Maybe I should try some of those dementia tests you can do at home."

"She's fine mum, just preoccupied I think. Let's go help her with dinner, give us something to do" Kate replied as she hooked her mums arm and steered her towards the kitchen where they could hear pans banging and some swearing, Peggy's normal kitchen routine.

Chapter 21

Ellie and Gavin were once more walking through the corridors of the medical wing at Barlinnie. Sandra, the night shift nurse was on and seemed happy enough to answer their questions when they called earlier.

Gavin went off to meet with the senior prison officer in order to review the CCTV of the medical wing as Ellie carried on into the ward itself. The good Doctor had his door closed tonight which suited Ellie, she didn't think he knew anything anyway. She turned towards the beds to spot a tall woman taking bloods from a patient and laughing at something he was telling her. Ellie waited until she was finished with her patient before catching her attention.

"Sandra? I'm Detective Superintendent McVey, we spoke earlier?"

"Ah yes, you said you were coming in. Would you like a cuppa hen? I'm gasping for one."

Ellie politely refused but followed Sandra into the

little kitchen as she made herself a cup.

"Sandra…when we were here yesterday, one of your colleagues told us that you are never ill." Ellie began

"That's true, strong constitution my dad always said" Sandra said proudly.

"Well don't you think we would find it strange that on the first night in years, you call in sick, and then a prisoner escapes…" Ellie left that question to hang in the air as Sandra realised the implication and went pale.

"Oh no hen…it's not…I mean…" Sandra started babbling and then sighed and looked straight at Ellie. "I wasn't sick ok? I won a competition, weekend break up in Pitlochry but the catch was that I needed to go right then."

"Who told you this?" Ellie asked.

"The wee woman on the phone. She called and said she was from the bank nurse agency and that I had won one of their annual prizes. So I says to her, I've not entered any prize draws and then she says that our employee numbers get drawn. So I tell her that I'm on shift that night and couldn't possibly drop everything and go. That's when she tells me not to worry, just call in sick and tell them that you've arranged someone to cover the shift. They said they would get one of the bank nurses to work the shift and I could get a nice spa break. Well it's been that long since I've had a break…I knew I shouldn't have lied but I didn't think there was any harm in it." Sandra finished her confession and sipped at her tea.

"Did your spa weekend turn out as expected?"

"Oh yes it was marvellous, everything paid for up front so I had a nice massage and the food was to die for." Sandra perked up at being able to talk about her holiday.

"Can you tell me what agency it was that called you and if you know the name of the caller?"

"Now I'm sure she told me her name...but I'm rubbish at remembering them hen. Although I don't think she said what agency now you say it... she just said the bank agency and I never thought to ask more. I've got the number here though if that helps? It was my mobile they called." Sandra scrolled through to find the call and showed Ellie the number and she noted it down to get Simpson to trace it.

Ellie finished with Sandra, promising not to tell her boss that she 'pulled a sickie' unless she needed to for the case. She went to meet Phil Hastings before he left for the evening. He was packing his briefcase as she entered the office.

"Oh hello, you're here late" he said with a smile. "Have you got everything you need?"

"Actually no, I'm having trouble locating the prison officer who escorted Cotton in the ambulance. Could you give me a name?" Ellie asked as she sat down and then she saw a hint of panic in his eyes.

"Well…you see that's where we are having a bit of an issue. Everyone on shift is accounted for and no one left to go in an ambulance. I've had every one of them in and their whereabouts for the time of the ambulance journey has been checked with CCTV, logs and witnesses. Our staff have to scan their passes in and out when they leave, even on escort duty and no one left."

"Are you telling me that a person unknown to you, dressed as a guard, escorted a whole life order prisoner?" Ellie was enraged at the laxity of the security.

"I wish I had an explanation for you, god knows it would make my life easier! I'm going to have to go in front of the select committee and explain this. I can't! I have no idea who went with Cotton but it was no one on staff, no prison officer set foot in the medical wing that evening."

"Looks like it's up to me to sort that out isn't it?" she said quietly as she left, swearing to herself that it wasn't just the good doctor that was being reported by the time she finished this.

She met up with Gavin in the CCTV control room as he was huddled over a screen with a Prison Officer.

"Ah ma'am just in time, this is Officer Black, he's

been reviewing the footage with me." Gavin said almost solemnly. Ellie nodded curtly, she knew that Gavin called her ma'am only when there was an anti-feminist to be dealt with.

"We've found the footage of the ambulance crew arriving and leaving, no joy though, they were wearing woolly hats low over their heads and kept their faces away from the cameras." Gavin explained. "There was something strange though, if you look, three ambulance crew went in, and only two came out."

"Yes but now there's a prison officer of a similar build to the missing ambulance crew, play that back." Ellie instructed. They watched again and it confirmed that the smallest of the ambulance crew became the prison escort on the way out. No faces could be seen throughout.

"So they knew where the cameras were then and it explains the mystery of the prison officer that wasn't there. The Governor will be pleased" she said sardonically. What about this bank nurse, did you find footage of her?" Ellie asked.

"Yes, just as you came in but look for yourself." Officer Black muttered.

Ellie watched the footage as the nurse walked around but always managed to keep her back to the camera. All they could tell was that she was young, slim and blonde.

Once they were alone Ellie put her thoughts to

Gavin.

"Complete inside job, it would be near impossible to walk around here without getting your face on one of the cameras, unless you studied the positions and planned well. How the hell did Cotton get these people to do this?" Ellie asked.

"Blackmail?" offered Gavin.

"Unlikely, Cotton had to put his trust in these people, and they did too good a job for it to have been forced on them. They wanted to help him… we need to track his visitors."

Chapter 22

Ellie and Gavin traipse through the door exhausted and frozen as it had started to rain. Their coats are dripping onto the floor as the dogs run to greet them.

"Oh, for goodness' sake you'll catch your death!" Peggy ran towards them fussing.

"Oh, let me get that coat off you, now I've made you some stew I know that's your favourite. Now you sit down, and I'll bring you a plate and a nice cup of tea." Peggy carried on as she fussed over Gavin, hanging his coat up and leading him off towards the kitchen. Ellie watched this bemused, still dripping on the floor.

"No don't mind me, I'll just catch pneumonia or consumption!" Ellie shouted towards the kitchen as she heard a chuckle. Kate walked through from the kitchen and takes Ellie's coat off her.

"Poor baby" Kate jokingly soothed as she hung Ellie's coat up and then kissed her nose.

"Thanks sweetie...at least someone cares!" Ellie

shouted towards the kitchen.

"Oh, stop moaning Eleanor, your wife is here to fuss over you so why do you need me?" came the curt response.

"Charming" muttered Ellie as she put her arm around Kate's waist and walked towards the kitchen. "Good to see I'm valued around here, could be dead in a ditch but so long as her little prince is ok…"

Ellie sits down at the kitchen table, giving Gavin a sour look as he gave her a smug grin with a mouth full of stew. Kate placed a bowl of stew and a cup of tea in front of Ellie and sat down beside her as Peggy continued to fuss in the kitchen. Aggie walked through from the hallway looking distracted, she quickly pocketed her phone once she realised everyone was there.

"Hello everyone, full house at last? Ellie, you look half drowned! Why has no one got you a towel?"

It was Ellie's turn to look smug as Aggie rushed towards the drier and pulled out a warm fluffy towel to drape over Ellie's sodden shoulders. "At least my mother-in-law loves me." she muttered into her stew as Kate elbowed her in the ribs.

"Stop being so melodramatic dear it doesn't suit a woman of your height." said Peggy as she sat down with a cup of tea and pursed her lips.

"Oh I'll be going out shopping tomorrow

afternoon everyone, just in case you wonder where I've gone." Aggie said in a light tone but Peggy drew her a suspicious look.

"Shopping? For what? We're supposed to be in lockdown from a potential fruit loop killer!" Peggy cried. "What on earth is so important?"

"I need new shoes." Aggie said simply but with a tone that clearly stated, 'don't question me'.

"How did your interviews go today?" Kate asked quickly before war erupted.

"Well, our visit was definitely illuminating." Ellie responded with a mouth full of stew. "Sandra, the night shift nurse, confessed that she wasn't really sick but was told to call in by the bank agency so that she could claim their prize draw holiday."

"Oh lovely, where did she go?" asked Aggie excitedly.

"Hardly the point Aggie dear." Peggy shushed her.

"Well excuse me for being happy for someone's holiday" muttered Aggie into her tea as Peggy shushed her again.

"CCTV also shows that the ambulance crew and the nurse brought in by the agency as a replacement, all hid their faces from the cameras." Gavin added as he slid his empty bowl away. "And then one of the ambulance blokes changes into prison guard gear and acts as the prisoner escort on the way out."

"Hmm…that should be almost impossible to do in a prison environment." Peggy mused.

"I agree, there had to be some meticulous planning involved and a lot of outside help." Ellie added.

"Who would help a monster like him?" shuddered Aggie.

"Oh, mum you would be surprised! Think of Ted Bundy or Richard Ramirez, they had legions of female admirers even during their trials!" Kate said.

"Aye but Ted Bundy was a good-looking boy, yer man Cotton looks like the Penguin from the batman film!" Aggie exclaimed.

"Ted Bundy was a good-looking boy?" Kate asked her mum in shock.

"Well…no…but I mean compared to all the others…" Aggie back tracked.

"So, its ok for these women to fan-girl over a serial killer because he doesn't look like Freddie Krueger or a thumb with eyes?" Kate rolled her eyes.

"Be that as it may" Peggy intervened. "You are working on the assumption that Cotton has friends and that those friends are the ones who freed him?"

"Yes, that's what we think for now and that's where we are starting tomorrow, going through everyone who visited him or stayed in contact with him." Ellie said with a yawn.

"Well, I think we should all get some rest, it's been a long day." Aggie said with a finality that nobody argued against, and they all headed to their rooms.

Chapter 23

The rain was still torrential as Ellie and Gavin got to work the next morning.

"I swear I need to get myself some better boots, if I keep wearing these, I'm gonnie end up wi trench foot." grumbled Gavin as he sat down at his desk and took off his shoe to look for holes.

"Diddums" was Ellie's sarcastic response as she sat down at her own desk, she hated rainy days, why she moved to Scotland she'll never understand.

"Just cos I'm Peggy's favourite." he teased as she chucked a file at his head.

Simpson ducked just in time as the file sailed back towards Ellie and she carried on professionally as if nothing happened.

"Ma'am I have the visitor list that Harris was working on, there aren't many, six in fact. I have names and addresses for them all."

"Excellent, thanks Simpson, we'll make our way through our half of them today. Give the other half to Kent to check. Has anything else come in overnight?" Ellie asked.

"Yes ma'am, forensics have been through PC Harris' phone, and they believe that he met Cotton on the Tinder app. They've found messages between the two accounts arranging to meet for the night he died. Harris…um…he put on his dating profile that he worked in the Major Crimes Unit…." Simpson tailed off as Ellie and Gavin digested this information.

"I told him never EVER to put where he worked on those sites!" cried Kent from her desk, her face flushed with anger. "Now look what's happened!" Kent rushed out, punching the wall as she left.

"Do you think Cotton targeted Harris then?" Gavin asked quietly.

"I think Cotton will have been trolling the app anyway, looking for a man to 'save'. He wouldn't have been able to resist once he saw where Harris worked… that's why he took that picture, he knew we would see it." Ellie explained, bile rising in her throat at the glee Cotton would have felt when he saw Harris' profile.

"That bastard" growled Gavin. "He killed Harris for sport, to mess with us rather than for some twisted mission."

"I agree, whatever mission Cotton was on before, he just enjoys it now. We need to find him Gav, no one is safe until we do. Let's see we have, Jamie

Fulton, Leah Houston, and Cotton's aunt Jacqui to see. I suggest we make a start. Simpson…could you make sure Kent is ok?" Ellie asked as she got up.

"No problem ma'am, I'll give her a few minutes to cool down and then I'll bring her a cuppa." Simpson replied with a sad smile.

Chapter 24

Ellie and Gavin arrive at the first address on Simpson's list. Jamie Fulton lived in a tenement flat just off Queen Margaret Drive, popular with students. They are buzzed in to the main close and head up to the first floor and were greeted at the door by a handsome young man, like *really* handsome! Ellie knew she wasn't the best judge of such matters but he looked like some Greco classical statue. He was tall, blonde, very muscular with perfect teeth and a warm smile. He introduced himself politely.

"Good morning, are you the people from the Police? Please come in, would you like something to drink? Herbal tea perhaps?" he carried on as they followed him into a bright airy flat. To say it was minimalistic would not do the place justice. It was like a white painted cell. As Jamie offered them the only seat in the flat (a low futon style sofa) he went off to the kitchen to make tea. Gavin attempted to sit down but the futon was so low that he ended up just falling with style. He scrambled into a sitting position, his long legs up at his ears.

"How does he sit on this?" he whispered as he gave up and just sat cross legged on the floor. "Look at this place, it looks like when star trek visits one of those planets that have more evolved societies, you know where they wear togas and speak in riddles." Gavin said knowingly. Ellie nodded having no idea what he was talking about.

Jamie came back into the room carrying a tea tray with three tiny cups and a small teapot. He made quite the drama of pouring the tea like he was a geisha engaging in the tea ceremony. He handed them each a cup and, out of politeness, Ellie took a sip and nearly spat it straight out. She had never tasted a herbal tea like it, but she was convinced it was essence of mould. She set the cup gingerly down on the floor as Jamie sipped his own horrid brew delicately.

"Mr Fulton" she began.

"Jamie, please I insist" he said with a smile.

"Jamie, we're here today to ask you about your association with an inmate at Barlinnie prison."

"Oh of course, How can I help? I'm a Youth worker for a drugs charity so I tend to meet a lot of ex-prisoners"

"Well this inmate you met in prison, you visited him and he is too old for you to have met with him in a youth work capacity." Ellie responded.

"What is this man's name?" Jamie asked as he finished his tiny cup of rotten tea.

"John Peter Cotton. You visited him four times at Barlinnie in the past six months." Gavin answered, reading from the notes that Simpson had provided.

"Ah yes John, such a nice man. What can I help you with?" Jamie replied serenely but Ellie noticed that his smile was a little more forced than it was previously.

"Well I guess the first question would be, how do you know Cotton?" Ellie asked.

"Oh I don't know him."

"But you visited him."

"Yes I did."

"Sir...can you explain yourself please?" Ellie was getting irritated by this hippy dippy serene nonsense and her back was starting to hurt sitting on a futon after the age of 22.

"Yes I visited John, but I didn't know him. I visit inmates in prison as part of the work my church does." He replied.

"I see, what church do you go to?"

"Seven Towers church. Is there anything else officers?" he asked, now keen to bring this interview to a close.

"Yes I have a question. You said you visit inmates as part of the church work, can you tell me who else you've visited in prison?" Gavin asked as he hauled himself to his feet.

"Well…you know I don't think I can remember any of the others. Isn't it funny how the mind works." he simpered.

"That's all for now Mr Fulton, we may want to speak to you again so don't make any plans to leave the country anytime soon." Ellie warned as they walked down the white hallway and back into the close.

<h1 style="text-align:center">Chapter 25</h1>

The second name on the list was Adam Rafter. His address was in the student heart land of Murano Street. Gavin knocked on the door and when it opened, was nearly knocked out by the fumes of stale beer and smoke that emanated from the flat.

"Adam Rafter?" Ellie asked as she showed her badge to the tall young man who answered the door with what looked like a gale force hangover wearing a spongebob onesie.

"Naw, he'll be in his room praying for our souls no doubt" he muttered rolling his eyes and then regretting it, he swayed a little as he held his head like it might shatter into a million pieces.

"Don't suppose you brought a greggs or something with you?" he asked hopefully.

"I'm afraid we don't deliver hangover food anymore son, cutbacks." Gavin explained as the walking hangover nodded dumbly. "Oh aye… suppose so. Anyway Saint Adam will be in the last room on the left. You'll need to knock cos he locks it, scared what we'll do during one of our hedonistic parties. Dunno why he chose to live in a student flat, he doesn't do any of the student things." He complained.

"Does he study?" Gavin asked.

"Aye, if he's no at church he's studying."

"Then he's doing what a student is supposed to do." Gavin said simply. The hangover took one look at him and then shook his head, regretting it.

"Were you born this old or did you just get loads of practice?" and with that he stalked off towards the living area.

"Did you hear that? Cheeky wee sod." Gavin was affronted.

"Well be fair…what do you remember about your student days?" Ellie asked.

"Well…I mean…let's not get into that right now, the point is that these kids should be knuckling down to their studies." He said evasively.

"Uh huh…that's what I thought" chuckled Ellie as they reached Adam's room. She knocked on the door and he opened it within a few seconds. Even though he was expecting them, he still looked surprised when he opened the door to them. No doubt he was expecting his less than studious flatmate.

"Hi Adam, one of your flatmates let us in, ok if we come in to talk?" Gavin asked brightly.

"Huh, those heathens, I can't wait to get out of here and away from them. It's like Sodom and Gomorrah in here." He muttered.

"Oh are you planning on moving then?" Ellie asked as she sat down at a small desk.

"Well no…not really…just thinking maybe for next year…" he said evasively.

"Well now Adam we're here to discuss a prisoner that you used to visit regularly, John Cotton, can you tell me why you visited him?"

"Oh yes, John is a friend of mine from church." Adam said simply.

"But…surely once he was convicted of murder…" Gavin began.

"He who is without sin cast the first stone" Adam intoned.

"Aye that's all well and good if someone shoplifted or cheated at cards but Cotton's a serial killer!" Gavin was incredulous.

"Some call him a monster, others as a saviour." Adam said quietly.

"What do you mean?" Ellie caught on the point.

"Just that some would say that the people he killed…well…they were sinners weren't they?" Adam shrugged.

"So you don't think he should be in prison?" asked Gavin.

"Oh he should, it's the law, I understand that. I'm just telling you what some people might think." Adam said, a smile returning to his face.

"Now if you don't mind, I've got a lot to do, exams and so on." Adam stood to end this meeting.

"Of course, what is it you're studying anyway?" Ellie asked.

"I'm training to be a paramedic."

"Isn't that interesting DI Bickerton?" Ellie asked as she noticed that Adam was quite small in height, much like the Prison escort from the CCTV images.

"Very Ma'am" he responded as they left knowing exactly who came to get Cotton that night.

"Oh one more thing, what church do you attend?"

"Seven Towers on Byers Road" he said as he closed the door on them.

Next stop on the list was to a woman called Leah Houston. They pulled up to the address Simpson had given them, not too far away on Gibson Street. Once again they were buzzed into the main close and walked up the two floors this time to Leah's flat.

"I swear if this lassie has a futon I'm leaving" muttered Gavin as they knocked the door and waited.

Leah Houston was perfume advert beautiful. She

was willowy, blonde and in her mid-20s. She answered the door bare footed and serene.

"Good morning, can I help you?"

Ellie was first to recover, Gavin was still openly staring at her.

"Yes..ahem…good morning, I'm Detective Superintendent McVey, we spoke on the phone?"

"Oh of course, I'm sorry I forgot, I was meditating and lost all track of time. Please come in."

The mention of meditation had Gavin on the lookout for more futon business but his relief was visible when they were shown in to a bright living room with a comfy looking sofa which she offered to her guests. Leah then plopped herself lightly down into a bean bag 'what is it with young folk and uncomfortable seating arrangements?' Ellie thought to herself.

"Ms Houston, we would like to ask you about you visiting an inmate at Barlinnie prison."

"Yes, dear John. Lovely man" she said lightly.

"By dear John, are you referring to John Peter Cotton?" Gavin asked, shocked at the warmth in her voice for a serial killer.

"Why yes of course. I've visited John several times, I'm so blessed." She said dreamily.

"Did you know him before he went into prison?"

Ellie asked.

"No, I only met him through visiting."

"Why did you visit him? Is it through your job?"

"Oh no, that would be silly." She giggled and Ellie had never heard a laugh so unnerving. "I'm just qualified as a teacher. No I visited him because of the church."

Alarm bells started ringing as Gavin shared a look with Ellie.

"What church do you go to may I ask?" Gavin said.

"Seven Towers. They asked me to visit so I did, and I'm so glad I did, John is such a good man, he's been doing the Lord's work." she said robotically as the hair on Ellies neck stood up.

Chapter 26

Ellie and Gavin got as far away from Leah Houston's flat as possible, both unnerved by the way she spoke about Cotton. They parked up at Cotton's aunt Jacqui's house before they spoke.

"That was without a doubt, the single most freaky thing I've experienced outside of a horror film." Gavin decided.

"Agreed, all that Lord's work business. It gave me the fear." Ellie admitted. "What do you make of this church?"

"It can't be a coincidence that three people who visit Cotton come from the same church and seem a bit…" Ellie couldn't find the words.

"Like they're part of a children of the corn style cult that should have its own Netflix special?" Gavin finished her thought.

"Aye…that." Ellie agreed as they took a breath to ready themselves for round three. Jacqui Cotton lived in an adapted bungalow for the elderly, three streets away from the Western Necropolis. Ellie had forgotten that little fact until they pulled up outside. Jacqui was elderly, much older looking than when Ellie last saw her at the trial. She answered the door holding on to a stick for support.

"Good afternoon Mrs Cotton, do you remember us?" Ellie asked gently.

"Oh yes dear, you're a police lady. You were here to talk about John before he was taken to prison." She said not unkindly.

"Yes that's me. Would you mind if we came in to talk about John more?"

"Oh no I wouldn't mind that at all. She shuffled ahead of them into a small sitting room. Gavin offered to make the tea and made himself busy in the kitchen leaving Ellie alone to talk.

"I forgot to offer my condolences for John's passing." Ellie began.

"Oh dear you must be mistaken, my John isn't dead, oh no, I only spoke to him yesterday. No dear you must have him mixed up with someone else…maybe it's the person who did all those awful things that John was accused of?" She asked, her eyes wide an innocent.

"But…the prison contacted you to claim his body." Gavin said as he walked in with the tea things.

"Not me, dear, I might be old but I've still got my faculties. No one from that dreadful place has phoned this house." She was adamant. Ellie decided to move on with the questions as Jacqui was sure of her answer to the first and they would have to deal with the truthfulness of her statement at a later time. Her guess was that the next of kin details had been changed to someone else so that his aunt never got the call about his alleged death. If Cotton could arrange a nurse, paramedics and prison guard then a simple bit of paperwork was hardly going to be an issue.

"Do you miss him?" Ellie asked.

"Oh yes, such a good Christian boy. He would never let me carry the messages or do the hoovering. He's so popular too, always with lots of friends."

This was news to Ellie and Gavin, everyone they had spoken to during the original case had described Cotton as quiet, shy and 'creepy with the Jesus stuff'.

"It's nice to have friends" Ellie said with a smile. "Where did John meet his friends?"

"Oh at his Church, good Christian boys and girls. A lot of the time they would come back with him here and visit in his workshop." Jacqui said as she helped herself to some shortbread off the plate offered by Gavin.

"I'm sorry, his workshop?" Ellie sat up quickly. What workshop?"

"The one at the bottom of the garden silly, John used to fix peoples computers for them in there. I never go in there, that's his space but that's where he would take all his friends, oh they would be in there for hours, I would leave tea and sandwiches outside the door. There was even a young lady amongst his friends, oh she was devoted to him. In fact she still comes to visit me to bring me shopping and to tell me all the news from John after she's visited him. Jessie her name is, lovely lassie. But they always met at the workshop."

'How in the hell did we miss a workshop and who is Jessie?' Was the thought running through Ellie's mind like a train.

"Would you mind if we took a look at his workshop?" Ellie asked, keeping the urgency out of her voice.

"Well…I don't know…John would be so cross if someone was in disturbing his things…" Jacqui said unsure of what to do.

"Oh don't you worry Mrs Cotton, I promise we won't touch a thing so he needn't be cross" Gavin said gently with a smile. His charm seemed to do the trick and Jacqui agreed. She led them down to the end of the garden and then through a gap in the hedge to reveal a large summer house. She unlocked the door and then left them to it, she didn't want to miss Countdown.

"That's how we missed it, the bloody thing's hidden!" Ellie grumbled. "You ready?" she asked as she grasped the handle.

"Not at all" Gavin said as she opened the door and they walked inside. Whatever they were expecting, it wasn't this.

They were standing in the middle of a chapel. There were twelve chairs arranged to face one large, ornate throne. Behind the throne were photographs, Ellie walked towards them to have a look. The photos were of all of Cotton's victims and their alleged sins. What scared Ellie the most was that Harris' picture was on here too. Cotton had been here since escaping prison. Jacqui hadn't been lying when she said she spoke to him yesterday. He had been here!

Chapter 27

Back at the office the team regroup after the interviews. Kent had managed to get round her three quickly as two of them lived together in student accommodation and the other lived only two streets away.

"Well to say the least, today was very...um...illuminating?" Ellie said, unsure of how to word it.

"With respect ma'am, I think the words you need right now are fucking disturbing." Kent piped up and Gavin agreed, nodding his head.

"Well...aye...I can't argue. I take it your interviews were as strange as ours?"

"Yes and I can't put my finger on why, they were all polite young people...it's just they were a bit... I don't know..." Kent was struggling for words and Gavin helped out.

"Children of the corn cult?"

"Yes! Thank you! I mean two of the lads were gorgeous, like from American telly gorgeous and the girl was too. I felt uneasy in their company and I couldn't put my finger on why."

"Yes I must admit our first three were exactly as you described Kent, but that creepiness was nothing compared to what we found at Cottons aunts. Gav, get the video up you took on your phone." Ellie said as she moved to the side and Gavin cast his phone to the tv. It showed the chapel, the 12 chairs, the throne and the photos. Kent gasped when she saw Harris on there.

"So what do we think?" Ellie asked as the video ended.

"That cult is the right idea" muttered Simpson looking horrified. "The twelve chairs...does that mean disciples?" she asked.

"Yes that would be my guess. I think that Cotton has brainwashed twelve people to be his disciples and I can guarantee he met them at that Seven Towers church. If he has managed to convince twelve people that his mad perversion of the scripture is the true faith, then they have to be the people he would turn to when he hatched his escape plan. We need to visit that church and see what the hell is going on in there." Ellie said as Simpson walked to her desk.

"On it ma'am, getting the address, service and Pastor details for the church, I'll send it to your phone."

"Brilliant, thanks. We'll head over there once we know there's a service on."

"There's a prayer gathering tonight ma'am" Simpson said as she scrolled quickly through their social media pages. "It says here they hold them nightly and all are welcome."

"Excellent, oh Simpson, see if you can run down a Jessie in all the stuff connected with Cottons visitation list. His aunt seems to think she was 'devoted' to him"

"I'll get on it ma'am"

"Right everyone go home and get some rest, bright and early tomorrow. Tonight your boss and Gavin are going to church." Ellie said as Gavin groaned.

"Why are you interested in this Jessie by the way?" Gavin asked.

"Because if we are right in the fact that he has twelve disciples, well twelve people didn't visit him did they? There is no Jessie on our list and his aunt said she would give her the gossip when she went to visit him. How did she visit? Surely her name would have popped up on the visit list? I think that Cotton needed one faithful right hand man, to pass his messages to the rest of his flock and to coordinate them all. Who would be better than his most devoted?" Ellie said.

"Bloody hell aye, I never picked up on that. We need to find that out." He agreed.

Chapter 28

Ellie and Gavin park up on Byers Road and walk towards where Simpson had said the address was.

"This is a church?" Ellie asked dubiously as they finally found a sign for Seven Towers in a dingy back alley off Ashton Lane. The door was almost hidden behind a pub's bins and the entrance to a bookies. They open the door and walk up the stairs that had the most stained and dubious looking carpet Ellie had ever seen.

"It's sticky!" Gavin hissed disgustedly as he gingerly picked his way up the stairs.

They could hear music coming from the rooms upstairs and followed the sound. They walked into a large room full of people with their eyes closed and their arms raised swaying to the music. Ellie didn't recognise the song but from what she heard of the lyrics it seemed to be some modern 'Jesus Tune'.

Ellie scanned the room and noticed something, she nudged Gavin. "Have you noticed that we are the oldest people in here?"

"Aye you're right, I don't see anyone over 25 here" muttered Gavin.

"And every one of them looks like a model, how in the hell did Cotton mix with these people and get them to follow him?" Ellie whispered back. "He's small, overweight, balding with a ponytail and looks like the penguin!"

Their confused musings were interrupted when a side door opened, and a tall, tanned man walked through. He noticed the newcomers straight away and focused a dazzling smile on them and walked towards them.

"Hi there, welcome to our little flock" He oozed with an American accent. He shook hands with Gavin and when he shook Ellies, he didn't let go and pulled himself awfully close. Ellie took a step back and introduced herself. At the mention of her rank, he immediately let her hand go and remained at more of a distance. On closer inspection the man was older than he looked from afar, he was attempting to freeze time with botox and fillers.

"How can I help Scotland's finest? I'm the pastor here, Dexter Saltire." He said with a flourish.

'That name has to be fake' thought Ellie as he started to show them around the room.

"How long have you been Pastor here Mr Saltire?" Ellie interrupted his sales pitch.

"I brought my ministry over to Glasgow fifteen years ago, been in this little room all that time. We mostly get students because of our proximity here to Glasgow Uni but all are welcome, we are a cosy flock" he added with a wink as Ellie's skin crawled. 'What a lech'.

"Was John Peter Cotton ever a member of your 'flock'?" Gavin asked, clearly unimpressed with Saltire. At the mention of Cotton, Saltire's tan seemed to fade a little.

"Ah yes John, yes he was a member of our congregation. He used to fix our computers and liked the place so much he started to attend regularly; he was very devoted."

"Was he popular here?" asked Ellie.

"Well…I wouldn't say popular…he was very quiet. But I do seem to remember that he liked chatting to a group of our members from time to time. I dare say they were even friends at one point. I know that young Adam Rafter spent time with him when he needed help with his pc for his studies and Jessie Taylor was always with him when he was here." He conceded.

"Jessie Taylor?" Ellie asked "Do you have an address for her?"

"Um…I don't think so, she started to turn up not long after John did but when asked for her details, she was always evasive. We didn't like to ask again, just in case the poor girl had trouble at home you see?" he said with a small smile.

"And as part of your ministry, do you encourage your members to visit inmates in prison?" Gavin asked.

"Oh goodness no, that would potentially place our flock in peril. My insurance wouldn't cover something like that" he added quietly. "No, we focus our outreach on youth groups and student bodies."

As he was talking Ellie noticed a group of people in her peripheral vision, they were watching her like hawks.

"May we have a list of your members? We may need to contact some of them regarding their links to Cotton." Ellie said, she made it sound like a command rather than a request and she was relieved that Saltire acquiesced almost immediately.

"Of course, we have nothing to hide officers. If you give me an email address, I will get it sent over to you directly." He flashed another winning smile at them, but Ellie and Gavin had already formed an ill opinion of the man. Gavin handed over his card, and they walked away. Once out of earshot Ellie muttered "Get Simpson to dig into him, everything she can find on him".

Chapter 29

Kate is pacing in front of her computer trying to figure out how her heroine gets out of the particularly deadly situation she has been written into. Kate can't see a way out and it's frustrating her. Bella has long given up pacing with her and was now snoring underneath the desk, but Bruiser was still full of enthusiasm for the task and dutifully trotted along at Kate's heels.

Peggy walked through the front door looking pensive, Kate however looked alarmed. "Why were you out alone?! Bloody hell have you forgotten that a serial killer is knocking about the place?!" she had stopped her pacing a little too abruptly for Bruiser whose face was instantly squished into Kate's leg.

"Hmmph don't you be getting at me Katherine Mitchell! I was perfectly safe, I took a surveillance team from work with me. Which is more than I can say for your mother!"

"What do you mean? Is mum not still down in her

room?" Kate looked alarmed.

"No, she skipped out, after she promised us, she wouldn't go shopping! I knew she was up to something so I followed her." Peggy explained.

"Oh, Peggy you didn't." groaned Kate. "And let me guess, she went shopping?"

"No…she didn't. She met that man of hers. They went into a building behind the Kings Theatre. My team and I stayed in the car park watching for over an hour until they came out again. Then they hugged and parted. That man went to get in a taxi and your mother walked off towards the city centre and into Buchanan Galleries, that's where I lost her."

"Peggy I'm seriously considering getting you some help, you're obsessed! Have you got nothing better to do? Is there not some politician that needs blackmailed or something?" Kate said in exasperation.

"Your mother has never lied to me, never kept things from me. I don't want her hurt again." Peggy said with feeling as tears filled her eyes.

"Peggy, I understand that you, in some way, blame yourself for mum's abusive past relationships. It wasn't your fault." Kate said as she took Peggy by the shoulders. "Mum is a grown woman who can make her own choices. Just be there for her, no more of this following her around, you're making yourself sick with worry."

Just then, the door burst open and Aggie fell through it roaring drunk and laughing her head off.

"Hellooooo family, I'm hooooooome!" she bellowed from her horizontal position on the floor.

"Agnes where on earth have you been?!" cried Peggy as she bent down to pick her sister up.

"I met a few of the girls from the WI when I was out...we have a few drinkypoos but then we had to leave because some spoilsport complained to the bar manager that we were being rowdy! Us!" she pointed at her chest in a melodramatic fashion. Peggy takes a chance.

"Where were you before that Aggie?"

"Before? I was tripping the fight lantastic" she slurred and then giggled at her joke before passing out.

"Fantastic" muttered Kate as the doorbell went. Peggy starts to half carry, half drag Aggie towards the bedrooms to sleep it off while Kate steps over her prone mother to get to the door as Peggy muttered something about "grown woman".

A tall young man was at the door in a high vis jacket and a clipboard.

"Good evening, sorry for the late delivery, we got delayed. I've got a signed for delivery for a Ms McVey?" he said as he held out a small brown envelope.

Just then she heard a bang and a crash behind her as Peggy misjudged where Aggie's legs were going and managed to get her hooked around a small end table and sent the plant standing on it flying. This briefly woke Aggie up.

"Whatreyoudoin…gerroff" she started to swat her hands about.

Kate needed to help so she turned back to the young man and signed for the envelope, dumping it on the table before running to help Peggy lift Aggie into bed.

By the time they got her settled, Kate and Peggy looked like they had been in a fight with a mountain lion. They came back to the living room just as Ellie and Gavin returned home.

"What happened to you two?" asked Ellie as she dumped her keys on the table.

"Mum had a drinking session with the women's institute" Kate explained as she sat down exhausted.

"Say no more" Ellie said with a grin, she remembered the last time that lot went out on the lash. They were barred for life from the hotel they met at.

"I'm going to go call Mhairi, see how the twins are doing." Gavin said as he walked off towards his room.

"Are you both ok?" Kate asked as she got up to kiss

Ellie hello.

"Yeah, we're fine, just tired…and that church is creepy as hell. I'm glad I'm home Ellie admitted as she wrapped her arms around Kate and breathed in her scent, nothing soothed Ellie more.

"I'm glad you're home too. I'll make you some coffee, oh and a letter came for you a wee while ago. It's on the table." Kate said as she walked towards the kitchen. Ellie went over to the table and sorted through the usual bills and pizza offers that made up their post and found the envelope. She opened it to find the death card and another Bible verse, Matthew 7:15. Ellie quickly googled the verse. 'Beware of false prophets, which come to you in sheep's clothing, but inwardly they are ravening wolves.'

"Shit, Gav! We've got another one!"

Chapter 30

It wasn't until 6am the following morning that the body was discovered by the cleaning crew starting their shift. Dexter Saltire had been hung on an upside down cross within his own church.

Ellie walked towards the body as Doc Brett was examining the scene. Ellie noted the red nails hammered through his flesh into the cross. Gavin watched as she walked around the cross examining every inch of the scene.

"What are you thinking?" he asked eventually.

"Well, the staging is a bastardisation of a crucifixion, the upside-down cross could be representative of Saltire being a 'false prophet' in Cottons mind." Ellie stopped and looked closer at the heavy wooden cross. "How much do you think Saltire weighed?" she asked.

"I dunno, he was a tall bloke…maybe about 16 stone?" Gavin answered.

"I would guess that too…and how much do you think this cross weighs? There is no way that Cotton subdued Saltire, nailed him to that cross and managed to lift it up into position without a lot of help." Ellie replied.

"Doc, do you mind if I try moving this?" Gavin asked.

"You can try, forensics have been over it already, but I should warn you, the cleaning staff already tried to move it to get him down and there's at least two away to hospital with strained backs. They couldn't shift it." Doc replied, her eyes still on the body.

"His disciples must have moved up from helping him escape to actively taking part in his killings. That would explain how he had the strength to do all this."

"Well Ellie this man was crucified alive and left to bleed out, he has a stab wound to the chest which pierced his lung. Death would have been slow and painful. Body temp and lividity estimate that he died around 11pm to midnight last night." Doc said as she stood up and took her gloves off.

"So, he died after the card was delivered to me… Cotton is baiting me." Ellie said.

"Els, we need to be careful; I agree he's baiting you, but I don't want you going anywhere alone right now. We go together, eh?" Gavin said gently.

"Don't worry big guy, I'm not in a rush to be made Cotton's pin cushion again. I just need to be smarter this time. We need to find his disciples;

they will be the weak link here. It's obvious that they told Cotton about our visit to the church almost immediately after we had been there. That card arrived at my house an hour after we left. That means that some of the disciples were at Church last night." Ellie said.

"No doubt the ones that were eyeing us up." Gavin agreed.

"I've got an idea…Simpson is the youngest and isn't officially connected to our team, so Cotton won't know about her. I say we get Simpson into this church today unofficially, but we can let Saltire's assistant know who she is."

"What would that accomplish?" Gavin asked confused.

"Well, we have the list that Saltire sent of his congregation, don't we?"

"Yeah, must have been the last thing he did… why?" Gavin asked

"Get it to Simpson. If these people are as tight a flock as they say, surely, they will all be here to pray for their Pastor…well the ones that didn't kill him will be, but maybe the disciples might stay away? If we get Simpson to take names aided by Saltire's assistant, of all who show up today, then we can compare it to the list and see who didn't show. That must be the quickest way to sort through them, right?"

"Actually…yeah…that's a brilliant idea boss lady" grinned Gavin.

"Not just a pretty face, eh?" she said as they went to find the assistant to set things up.

Chapter 31

They gather at the office, ready to pass on more information.

"Ok folks we've just been to the crime scene, the victim we met yesterday, Dexter Saltire. Kent did we get anything on him?" Ellie asks.

"Yes ma'am, Saltire was born and raised in Utah. Not much is known about his early life, presumably because he changed his name at some point."

"I would assume Dexter Saltire was not his real name, no" Ellie agreed and urged her to continue.

"Well ma'am we first hear of Saltire when he sets up his ministry in Utah in 1992. He had to leave 15 years ago though under somewhat of a cloud."

"What kind of cloud?" Ellie asked as she makes notes on the board.

"The accusations of overfamiliarity with the youth of his church kind of cloud." Kent responded.

"Knew he was a creep" muttered Gavin, "The way he held on to your hand? Creepy."

"The FBI were brought in eventually as the local sheriff was getting dozens of witnesses saying that the church was a cult and that they had been trying to get family members out of it for years. But by this point Saltire was long gone and setting up fresh in Glasgow. There's still a federal warrant out for him in Utah." Kent finished.

"What a Prince" muttered Ellie. "We know from the crime scene that there is no way Cotton could have carried this murder out by himself, Saltire and the cross weighed too much. Cotton always chose graveyards because the crosses were already there for him, saved a lot of work. This one, he needed help. Do we know where those kids we spoke to are?"

"No ma'am" responded Kent and Ellie whirled around.

"No?"

"No ma'am, uniform went round to their homes after you called about the body. All six of those kids have skipped, no answer at their houses and no signs of anyone inside. One of the neighbours says they saw Jason hurrying away with a backpack not long after he was interviewed and Adam Rafters flatmates said that he ranted at their immorality before grabbing a bag and leaving." Kent explains.

"Well at least we can assume that those six are the

first six disciples." Said Gavin as Ellie stared off in silence. "And this Jessie would be number 7"

"I don't get why he's changed his kill area, I mean if he always leaves the bodies in graveyards, why did he change with Saltire?" Kent asked confused.

"Because this one mattered more to him" Ellie said quietly before she left the room. Kent looked to Gavin in confusion.

"The only other time Cotton deviated from his routine was to go after Ellie. If he's done this now, it means he is decompensating; getting bolder, because he's getting near to his end game." Gavin explained.

"What is his end game though?" Kent asked.

"I have no idea, I think once we figure that out, we'll be able to find him." Gavin said but he kept his owns fears to himself. He worried that the end game had a lot to do with Ellie and he thought that she knew that too. He was interrupted from his thoughts by the phone ringing.

"DI Bickerton" he answered.

"Ah Sir it's Simpson. I thought you should know, six members of the congregation haven't showed at the church. The assistant said that there is no way they would miss prayers. He also said that the six people all worked with Cotton on some project to bring more youth to the church, in fact all twelve of these young people worked on the project with Cotton. The assistant didn't know the exact nature of it but they spent a lot of time in meetings at Cotton's home." Simpson explained.

"Brilliant, do you have the names?" Gavin asked as he grabbed a pen.

"I'll send them to you know Sir but the boss wanted me to track a Jessie? Jessie Taylor is one of the names that didn't turn up today."

"Good work Simpson." He hung up "Kent you're going to get six names, I want you to get addresses for each of them but prioritise a Jessie Taylor, split the list and get uniform over to pick them up. Boss we got a lead!!" he bellowed.

Chapter 32

It didn't take long to get uniformed officers out to each of the addresses. Reports were coming in from each patrol unit intermittently.

"This is Tango Oscar 3, Luke Hilton not at home, his mother said he packed a bag last night and said he was staying with friends."

"Tango Oscar 2, Jessie Taylor hasn't been at the halls of residence since this morning."

"Tango Oscar 6, Joel Drake's parents haven't seen him in days, said he was off on a retreat with the church."

Ellie listened to three more reports like this as she paced up and down. The rest of the team watched helplessly.

"They must be going somewhere!" growled Ellie. "Hang on, it would be hard to hide thirteen adults, they would need space and privacy. I want you all to split this list up and go through their lives with a fine-tooth comb, I want to know about any property that has a link to these twelve people or even to Cotton himself, focus on large remote buildings. Make it quick folks, if these disciples have left their lives to join Cotton then his end game must be happening soon."

The team scrambled to their desks to start going through property registers and Gavin walked up to Ellie to speak privately.

"Els...do you think he will come for you again?"

"I honestly don't know" Ellie admitted. "If I was to guess I would say his agenda with me has changed, he's enjoying showing me what he's doing, it's like he's seeking approval. Whether or not he still wants to kill me? I don't know...I'm worried for everyone else right now." She admitted.

The next few hours were spent trawling through the Registers of Scotland looking at every bit of land or property owned by the disciples or their family members. It wasn't easy as most of these people were young students so hadn't bought any property yet and most of their parents owned flats or small houses in Glasgow that wouldn't be able to house thirteen extra people without being noticed.

"Oh wait, ma'am I think I have something!" Simpson shouted and everyone ran to her desk. "Jessie Taylor, her family owns a farm to the north of Glasgow. According to registers they usually lease it to tenant farmers but at the moment it's unleased."

"Can you bring up an image?" Ellie asked. Simpson

went on to google maps and entered the details and up popped the image of a lonely farmhouse with storage barns.

"I think that would be ideal, look it's only a ten-minute drive out Balmore road from the Necropolis." Ellie noted. "Simpson what does Jessie Taylor look like?"

Simpson brought up Jessie's student ID. She was young, blonde and a student nurse.

"I think we've found our mystery night shift nurse" muttered Ellie. "Who would he trust with such a job other than his right hand woman. Yeah, I think this is where they're going to be. Notify SWAT where to go and let's go!" Ellie cried as the team ran after her out into the night.

Chapter 33

The 4x4s carrying SWAT and Ellie's team rumbled forward on a country road towards the farm. When they got within sight, they killed the headlights and parked up so that they could move on silently on foot.

"Captain Potter, take your team to the farmhouse and we will go to the barn. I'm hoping we can take them by surprise. Good luck" Ellie whispered into the darkness as Captain Potter nodded and sent his squad silently up the farm track towards the house. Ellie, Gavin, and Kent crept up the path on the right towards the barn.

As they got closer, they noticed lights were on in the barn.

"Ma'am" Kent whispered as she pointed to the side of the barn, Ellie spotted what she was pointing at, a transit van with lettering and an ambulance parked up along the side of the barn.

"Well at least we've got the right place" Ellie whispered as they moved closer. Occasionally, a member of the SWAT team would be momentarily reflected in the moonlight and allowed Ellie to track their progress, they were nearly at the door. Ellie and the team moved close to the barn and quietly opened the latch.

"SWAT are you in position?" Gavin whispered into his mic.

"Yes, ready when you are" came the response through everyone's ears.

"Now!"

Gavin shouldered the barn door and Ellie rushed through, checking behind it and along the sides. Kent was at her back training her weapon to the right. In the distance they could hear the farmhouse door being kicked in. It wouldn't be necessary to be quiet anymore. Ellie, Gavin, and Kent stood at the door, their weapons dangling loose from their hands as they took in the horror before them.

Lined up in neat rows were the twelve young people, the disciples of John peter Cotton, every one of them nailed to a cross. Their young faces pale in death and white foam crusting the corners of their mouths.

There was a small table in the middle of this scene and Ellie walked towards it. The death card was placed on the table along with another Bible verse.

"Gav, google Exodus 20:2-6" Ellie said quietly.

Gavin found the passage and read it out.

""I am the Lord your God, who brought you out of the land of Egypt, out of the house of slavery. "You shall have no other gods before me. "You shall not make for yourself a carved image, or any likeness of anything that is in heaven above, or that is in the earth beneath, or that is in the water under the earth. You shall not bow down to them or serve them, for I the Lord your God am a jealous God, visiting the iniquity of the fathers on the children to the third and the fourth generation of those who hate me, but showing steadfast love to thousands of those who love me and keep my commandments."

"What the hell does this have to do with him killing twelve of his friends?" Kent asked, her eyes wide in horror still at the gruesome scene before them.

"It means he's punishing them. They worshipped Cotton, he's a false God." Ellie said simply.

"Sick bastard." Kent whispered.

"SWAT we've found twelve bodies in the barn. Let us know if there is any sign of Cotton. Consider him armed and extremely dangerous." Ellie ordered. "I better call forensics and Doc Brett out. You two check this place, see if there's anything to indicate where this bastard will go." Ellie said as she picked up her phone and dialled.

"Doc, I'm going to need you and basically everyone

you can spare. We've got twelve murders at this scene." Ellie said simply.

"Bloody hell, are you all ok?"

"Yeah…they were dead before we got here. I'll send you the address, it's a farmhouse so make sure you've got a 4x4 or you won't make it up the track."

"You got it Ellie, I'll be there soon." Doc said and hung up.

"Ma'am!" yelled Kent "We've got one still alive!"

Chapter 34

An ambulance took Jessie Taylor to the Royal Infirmary within twenty minutes of being called. Gavin rode along with her to take her statement and to keep guard over her as she was still a suspect in Saltire's murder and Cotton's prison escape. Doc Brett arrived a few minutes after the ambulance and her team set up in the barn to process the scene. Ellie and Kent stayed on scene to help with forensics and to identify each of the victims.

Ellie walked up towards where Doc Brett was examining one of the bodies. She was studying the white foam on their mouth.

"Ellie, I think they ingested poison before being nailed up here." Doc said as she went to the next victim in the row and checked their mouth too. Ellie looked around for what could be the source, she eventually found a black bin bag full of plastic cups just behind the door.

"Do you think he made them drink it like Jim Jones

with the Kool aid style?" Ellie asked.

"I don't know, but I'm not seeing any defensive wounds here Ellie. Looks to me like they ingested it either willingly or unknowingly. I'm also not finding blood spatters around these nails; they were dead before he nailed them up here."

"So, he gives them all a drink, its poisoned, they die and then he takes his time nailing each one of them to a cross and then hauls the whole lot up?" Ellie didn't like it. "I still don't see how he had the strength, some of these lads are big healthy blokes. I think he still needed help."

"Maybe he kept one alive to help and then poisoned them last?" offered Doc Brett.

"That would explain why Jessie was still alive when we arrived, she could have been done later than the others. She is also the most likely to help him unquestioningly and, as a nurse, would possibly be able to instruct in the poison." Ellie conceded.

Kent walked up to them with photos and lists in her hands.

"Ma'am I've identified all of the victims, confirmed them with pictures we had of each of them."

"Right, Doc are you ok here? We've got twelve families to give bad news to tonight." Ellie said grimly.

"Of course, I've got a full team here, I'll notify

uniform when we're done." Doc said as she squeezed Ellie's shoulder. She didn't envy what she had to do for the next few hours.

Chapter 35

Kate was pacing once more in the living room. Ellie had just called to tell her what they had found and to warn them that Cotton was not at the farm and for everyone to stick together. She had lost signal soon after that and Kate had been trying to call her back with no success.

She went through to the basement rooms of apocalypse mansion and found Peggy watching snooker with her feet up and a dog on each side of her, perfectly content.

"I just got a call from Ellie, they found twelve bodies…Cotton isn't one of them. She's told us all to stick together for now. She's driving to each of the family homes to break the news." Kate said quietly.

"Those poor parents" Peggy said shaking her head. "I'll go tell Aggie, and then we'll have a nice cup of tea and wait to see what Ellie says when she comes home".

Peggy got up and Kate went to the small basement

kitchen area and put the kettle on. She heard Peggy shouting her from down the hall.

"Kate, was your mum upstairs?"

"No, I thought she was in her room?" Kate shouted back and then walked through. Peggy was standing in the middle of Aggie's room. "Her phone isn't here."

"Maybe she's went down for a swim, I'll got check the pool, you see if she's in any of the bathrooms." Kate said as she headed further down the hall towards the pool area. She looked around but no Aggie, the floor was dry, no one had been in here recently. Kate went back up the corridor to be met with Peggy looking alarmed. "She's not here!"

"Shit where has that woman got to?" exclaimed Kate. She dialled Ellie's number, but she must still have been in a no signal area. "Right, desperate times…Peggy, get on to your mob and get them to trace mum's phone." Kate said as she got her shoes and coat.

"Why didn't I think of that" muttered Peggy as she made a call. Within a few minutes she had the phone's location. "They say she's in the Community Centre over in Summerston, what the hell is she playing at?" Peggy said angrily. "If she isn't in mortal danger, I'm going to kill her so help me!" she said as she hopped about on one foot trying to get her trainers on.

Kate called Gavin; he might be able to get word to

Ellie she thought.

"Gavin, my mum's left without saying a word, we've traced her phone to Summerston Community Centre...we're worried she didn't go willingly..." she admitted.

"I'll be right there. Don't let Peggy go in without me!" he ordered and hung up.

It took them ten minutes to get to the Centre, they arrived to see no cars in the carpark and only one light on inside. Gavin arrived seconds after them, he must have done 70 the whole way there!

"Right, I'll go in and make sure it's safe. Wait out here" Gavin instructed.

"Am I buggery" muttered Peggy as she bodily lifted him out of the way and rushed through the door.

"Aggie?! Aggie are you here?!" Peggy called as she ran through the corridors towards the main function room where the lights were on. She burst through, closely followed by Gavin and Kate to find Aggie standing alone in the middle of the room...in a ballgown.

"What the f..." Aggie began.

"What are you doing here? We've been worried sick!" Peggy wailed as she grabbed her sister by the shoulders. Aggie looked flushed and then sighed.

"If you must know...I may have...when I had a few too many sherries...agreed to be part of the WI ballroom dancing team for a charity event...." She admitted.

"Wait what? Mum you can't dance." Kate said, confusion overtaking shock as her focus for that moment.

"Well, I know that!" snapped Aggie. "That's why I asked Eduardo from the hairdressers to give me lessons...he was a champion ballroom dancer when he was young." Aggie said with a smile.

"Listen this is all very illuminating but what does it have to do with you being here on your own at night when there's a serial killer on the loose?" Gavin butted in.

"Well Eduardo text me to say to meet him here for a final practice."

"Show me the message." Gavin said holding out his hand for her phone.

"This number isn't saved in your phone."

"Well, no, he didn't his own number to text me, look it says his phone died and was borrowing one." She explained as she pointed out part of the message. Kate was massaging her temples, her head about to explode.

"Mum...did it not occur to you that someone could have been impersonating him in order to get you alone?" she said with forced calm.

"Oh well really, who would bother? It's not like I'm some spy or royalty. Honestly you lot and your criminal minds."

"Ok how about you carry on this conversation back at home. I'm going to organise surveillance for outside here in case someone shows up. I'll get you all safely home and then I've got to get back…I left a suspect at the hospital." He admitted.

"Oh Gavin I'm so sorry!" Kate was horrified that they had dragged him away from work.

"It's ok, I called to get cover sorted when I was driving here, someone should be with them now. Come on, let's get out of here before some local busybody calls the police about the best dressed cat burglar in the area" he nodded towards Aggie.

Chapter 36

Ellie and Kent had just finished with Adam Rafter's family. It was heart-breaking to tell these good hard-working people that their only son and first in the family to go to university, had been murdered. Kent got a call on the hands free in her car.

"Ah Kent are you with the boss?" Simpson asked.

"I'm here, what's up Simpson" Ellie replied from the passenger seat.

"It was just to tell you ma'am that we couldn't get anyone to cover for DI Bickerton at the hospital, everyone is tied up at the moment so would you like me to go down?"

"What are you talking about? Why isn't Gav at the hospital?" Ellie asked concerned. It wasn't like Gavin to walk off from his duty.

"He said he was heading to an emergency, that's all we know." Simpson explained, worried that she had effectively grassed in her DI.

"Right...well he must have had a hell of a good reason to leave a suspect unsupervised. I'll go down to the hospital myself Simpson."

"Yes ma'am"

The call hung up and Ellie turned to Kent "Will you be ok going to these families without me?"

"Yes ma'am, I'll call family liaison and see if I can get one of them out with me. I'll drop you off at the hospital on my way." Kent confirmed as she turned off the road and headed instead towards the Royal.

Ellie walked down the ward corridor towards the nurse's station.

"Hiya, Detective Superintendent McVey, I'm here to supervise one of your patients, Jessie Taylor." Ellie said to the staff nurse on duty.

"Of course, she's down in room 6 just off to the left there."

"Thanks, has anyone been in since my colleague left?"

"No, visiting hours are over so we've not had anyone here except us." The nurse confirmed.

Ellie entered room 6 and was surprised to find that Jessie Taylor was conscious. She was sitting up in bed.

"Who are you?" she asked warily as Ellie sat down on the chair by her bed.

"I'm Detective Superintendent McVey, I was part of

the team that found you out in the barn. You're very lucky to be alive." Ellie said quietly.

"The Lord protects those of us that are loyal" she said piously.

"Does that include murderers?" Ellie asked bluntly. Jessie didn't respond, instead she bowed her head in prayer.

"Tell me what you remember?" Ellie changed tact.

"We were in the barn…John told us that we were to be God's chosen ones and we would be kings in the new world. He gave us all wine to drink in celebration. I got dizzy and then I woke up here."

"Do you know what Cotton…I mean John plans to do?"

"He said he would lead us all to the promised land but that he still had one lost lamb to welcome into the fold."

"Who is the lost lamb Jessie?" Ellie asked.

"I don't know, he would never say." She said "But I know he needed to do this to complete the work that the Lord set for him."

"Did the work include asking you to help murder your friends?"

"I didn't murder anyone. All of us knew that our faith would be tested and that death is the final glorious stage before salvation" she explained with a manic glint in her eyes.

Jessie said as she started to rub her stomach. "Could you please get a nurse, I don't feel too good" Jessie said as she started to shake. Ellie ran out of the room and down the corridor.

"Nurse, can you help Jessie, I think that poison may still be affecting her." Ellie explained, this stopped the nurse in her tracks.

"What poison? Ms Taylor hasn't been poisoned; we ran a tox screen on her when she got here." The nurse explained.

"Wait, what? All the rest were poisoned."

"Well, she wasn't, all she had was some superficial wounds to her hands from where the nails went in."

"Superficial?"

"Yes, the nails went into the webbing between her fingers, she was very lucky" the nurse explained.

"Oh she wasn't lucky, Cotton would never make that kind of mistake with those nails, she was never meant to die, only to appear that way."

"Oh god they set it up!" Ellie realised too late; she ran back to the room to find it empty. Jessie was gone.

Chapter 37

Gavin has the family home safe, and he is trying to get hold of Ellie, her phone keeps ringing out and he's concerned. She should be in an area with signal by now.

"Still nothing?" Kate asked nervously.

"No...I'll try Kent again, see if I have better luck. He did, Kent picked up on the third ring.

"At last! I've been trying to get you and the boss for ages! Where are you?" Gavin said as Kent answered.

"The boss is at the hospital. They couldn't get cover for you, so she went down herself. I dropped her off half an hour ago." Kent explained.

"Then why isn't she picking up her phone?" Gavin was worried. "I'll try the ward, see if I can through to her that way, thanks Kent." He hung up and dialled the hospital.

"Ward 8" the calm voice on the end of the line said.

"Hi, I'm DI Bickerton, I was there earlier with Jessie

Taylor but I had to leave, can you get my colleague on the phone please?" he said quickly.

"Oh, I'm sorry I can't love, your colleague ran out of here a few minutes ago. Jessie Taylor escaped her room, and she's went after her." The nurse explained.

Gavin hung up, fear hammering at his heart "Els not again!" he groaned as he tried to calm his mind down from the rising panic.

"What's wrong?" Kate asked, fearful at his expression.

"Jessie Taylor escaped; Ellie's gone after her. I need to get down there. Peggy you're in charge, all of you down to the panic basement until you hear from either me or Ellie, am I clear?" he ordered and they all knew he meant it as he rushed out of the room dialling on his phone.

"Kent I want you to get SWAT and meet me at the hospital, something is wrong and we need to find the boss."

"I'm on my way"

Gavin was about to leave but had a brain wave. "Peggy!" he shouted as he raced back to where he left them all. "Can you track Ellie's phone? You would be quicker than our lot." He explained. Peggy was already making a call as he ran from the house and into his car. As he drove towards the hospital all he could think of was that night when he stopped Cotton from killing Ellie, they had been lucky that night. He was making deals to every entity that they could be that lucky again tonight.

"Ellie I'm coming" he muttered over and over as he floored it on the back roads.

Chapter 38

Ellie was hunting for Jessie; she was angry at herself for not seeing earlier that Jessie had been a plant left by Cotton. Jessie was the organiser, the one who passed Cotton's ministry to the others, the one who organised them all to their tasks, the one who faked Cotton's heart attack and the one who faithfully helped him to nail each of those followers to a cross. Ellie had run down to security to view CCTV and was able to track Jessie down to the morgue. She raced down the stairs until she reached the basement level of the morgue. She tried to steady her breathing as she walked through the doors. The place was empty, the signs up stated that it was closed for refurbishment. Her heart was racing as she crept carefully forward in the dark. There was a light at the end of the corridor.

"Of course, I have to walk down a dark corridor in a closed off morgue." She whispered to herself. "I would be shouting at the telly if this was a tv show" she muttered. "And now I'm talking to myself" she ran her hands across her face 'get a grip' she inwardly chastised herself.

She was panicking and she knew deep down why, she knew who would be down here waiting on her...it was always going to be this way. She lifted her phone out of her pocket and pressed two buttons simultaneously. She hoped that Peggy was still monitoring their phones as she gathered her bravery and carried on towards the light.

She opened the door to the lit morgue to find Cotton standing in the middle of the room, clearly, he had been waiting for her. He smiled. Before she could take another step, she was grabbed from behind and a scalpel blade held to her throat. Jessie held her tightly and Cotton still stood smiling.

"My lost lamb has returned to me." he whispered.

Chapter 39

Gavin and the team are outside the hospital when Peggy calls him.

"Ellie's phone is still in the hospital main building" she says.

"Ok, it's a start. I want you all to start taking floors each to search for the boss!" he shouted to the team.

"Oh Gavin!" Peggy shouted to get his attention back. "Her emergency system has started pinging. She must have activated it, once I get into the system, I'll be able to listen to audio from wherever she is." Peggy explained excitedly as she sat at her computer and accessed Ellie's emergency tracker.

"Ok, put your speakers up to your phone, I want to be able to hear in case she says anything that helps find her." He says, pacing now. Peggy turns the volume up and places her phone close to the speaker, Ellie's voice comes through loud and clear.

"I'm the lost Lamb Cotton? I'm surprised, I thought that would have been Jessie...she really has been your most faithful disciple. Not many people would let someone crucify them simply to get to me." Ellie was calm, she knew that Jessie was twitchy behind her, and she didn't want to get her throat slit.

"Yes, you're my lost lamb…I couldn't carry on with my celestial journey with unfinished business. You were the sinner that I never got to save, I was thwarted by that thuggish underling of yours and locked up for doing God's work." Cotton carried on in his soft voice.

"Is that why you have help today? Why Jessie is holding a scalpel to my throat?"

"Insurance, just to make sure that your salvation finally does come tonight at my hands." Cotton responded.

Gavin hears this through his phone and radios to the SWAT team that there are two armed suspects currently holding Ellie. He was running down corridors checking every room "Where are you, Ellie?" he whispered to the Universe hoping she would get the information he needed.

"What I don't understand though, is why?" Ellie continued in her strong voice. Kate, Aggie, and Peggy were all listening too, none of them even daring to breathe loudly. "What do you hope to accomplish by 'saving' people?"

"My eternal salvation of course, I bring lost sheep back to the heavenly fold, I make them repent for their sinful ways. I shall be rewarded on high for what I have done." Cotton said with a glowing smile. "We will sit on the left side of Him in the promised land" he said as he smiled over to Jessie who was now crying with her delight. 'Oh god they truly believed that'. Ellie thought.

"Why are we in the morgue though? I thought a church or graveyard was your thing?" Ellie asked.

"The morgue" Gavin roared into the radio as he skidded to a halt and tore down another corridor towards the main stairway.

"Yes, I thought it would be more fitting, the world already thinks I'm dead and this is where I was supposed to be taken. I'm sure the Lord won't mind me being a touch theatrical now."

Ellie needed to keep him talking, she pinned all her hopes on Peggy and Gavin listening in and getting the information they needed. Cotton was pleased with himself, she needed to use that to stall him for a bit longer.

"It was clever, I'll give you that Cotton. You planted one of your disciples in the medical wing…I'm guessing Jessie here with her medical background?" when he nodded, she continued. "You then fake a medical emergency…"

"Oh no, we didn't fake anything. Oh, dear no, we created a real one. It had to pass muster in case Crippen the prison Doctor decided to do his job for once. No young Jessie here injected me with potassium just before raising the alarm. It stopped my heart and gave enough reason to call the ambulance. Of course, Jessie dialled out, Luke, Adam and Joel were waiting just outside Barlinnie in our ambulance and were there in minutes. Adam swapped into prison officer gear in case we were stopped at the gates. Once I was safely inside, they restarted my heart and brought me round. Adam has paramedic training. It wasn't pleasant but one must suffer for good works" he said.

Gavin reached the basement and ran as quickly and as quietly as he was able down the corridor where he could hear voices. Kent had caught up with him and was right at his back with armed response. They needed to figure out who was where in that room before they burst in. Armed response fed a fibre optic camera under the door and scanned the room. They spot Jessie three feet in front of the door holding Ellie with the scalpel and Cotton facing them two feet further away. Cotton was armed with a knife and a hammer. Gavin had his eyes firmly on Ellie, he noticed that Jessie was on tiptoes, she must have been a good six inches shorter than Ellie's tall stature. 'Ellie could disarm her in a heartbeat from that position...so why hadn't she?' he thought to himself. Then he realised "she's stalling for time for us to get into position to take Cotton" he whispered to the team, and they nodded. He smiled a little 'Ellie could never be a damsel in distress'.

"Well now I must say it's been pleasant but it's time." Cotton said, interrupting Gavin's thoughts. "My disciples have gone on ahead of me and once I cleanse you of your sins, Jessie and I will take the holy wine ourselves and follow on to our salvation." Cotton moved to the side to pick up a large wooden cross that had been propped against the wall. Just then Ellie heard a quiet tapping on a pipe. 'Good old Gavin, he's ready' she thought to herself.

As Cotton turned his back a little to set up his cross Ellie shouted "Now!" She brought her head back sharply and heard Jessie's nose break with a loud crack. She kicked backwards and buckled Jessie's knee before swinging around and pinning her to the ground. Jessie fought like a wildcat but Ellie's superior strength and size got the better of her. Gavin and the armed response had swarmed the room and thrown themselves at Cotton before he had time to move. Cotton was wailing loudly, his eyes wide and Jessie was groaning as her nose poured with blood. Kent cuffed her and led her away. Ellie took the phone out of her pocket and spoke to the people she knew needed to hear her. "Thank you Peggy, you're some wingman. We're all safe."

Kate, Aggie and Peggy burst into tears and laughter as the tension left their bodies. Kate had been clutching Aggie's arm so hard she had left marks and Peggy had snapped three pencils in half.

Cotton looked rabid as he was carried kicking and screaming away. When his eyes locked on Ellie he mustered all of his strength to stare through to her soul. "You're my lamb and I will come for you, one of these days you will meet with redemption and I will be there to deliver it."

"Get this freak out of here" bellowed Gavin as he hugged Ellie as if he hadn't seen her in a decade.

"Don't you ever do that to me again Els, this has taken years off my life" he joked into her hair.

"But your life would be so dull without me" she joked back as she held him tight, grateful to have a friend like him.

"How about you not getting into trouble so much that it'll put me in an early grave? That's not much to ask is it?" he asked as they turned to walk out of the morgue.

"No…but trust me, with Mhairi, your kids, Peggy and your aunt Janet, I'm waaaay down the list of people that will give you your first heart attack."

"Oh cheers for that Els, if I ever need a silver lining I know I can count on you!" he moaned as they walked up the stairs and finally to safety.

Epilogue

The trial of Glasgow's biggest serial killer in living memory was over before it began. John Peter Cotton never recovered from the mania induced from his failure to secure his 'lost lamb'. He was found unfit to stand trial by several independent Psychiatists. The trial continued in his absence and he was bound over to spend an unspecified amount of time in the secure hospital of Carstairs. His release from that institution would need to be agreed by the Home Office. He was housed in the secure wing of the hospital for the safety of others after he attacked several inmates. He was never to find his right mind again and was known to scream every night unless sedated.

Jessie Taylor got life imprisonment for the murder of Dexter Saltire, the participation in the murder of the eleven other disciples, aiding and abetting a prisoner in avoiding the law and various other charges. She can apply for parole after 25 years. She smiled as she was sentenced. Cotton's Aunt Jacqui was there to see her sentenced and waved sadly at her as they took her down.

The funeral for Harris took place two days after the arrest in the morgue. Ellie, Gavin, Kent and Simpson wore dress uniform and carried his coffin into the church. Ellie presented a flag and Harris' uniform cap to his mother and saluted her. Harris' pension and death in the line of duty payments would go to her and Harris' father.

The family had requested that everyone not in uniform should wear rainbow colours to celebrate their son's life. His sisters wore Rainbow dresses, Kate, Peggy, Aggie and Mhairi all wore the brightest of colours for a colourful life lived. Harris' local bar also led a dedication to him and announced that a fund had been set up in his honour and it was to help LGBT+ kids who had been thrown out by religious family members or who had been put through the horrendous ordeal of conversion therapy. The Alex Harris Trust would protect others and ensure that he would never be forgotten. Ellie had tears in her eyes when this was announced at the service, she couldn't think of anything more fitting as a tribute.

After the service they all went to the bar and raised a toast in his honour. His photo had been placed in a frame behind the bar, it was one of him in full Dolly Parton Drag from last years New Years Eve. Kent looked at it with happy tears.

"I picked that outfit for him" she said as Ellie stood

beside her.

"I got him the boobs" Gavin responded.

"Who do you think it was that taught him 9-5?" Ellie asked with a wink as she walked away leaving the others rooted to the spot in shock.

PC Simpson requested a transfer permanently to the Serious Crime Squad. Ellie agreed without hesitation as she had proven herself over this horrible time. She was now Detective Constable Gayle Simpson, no longer in uniform and she was proud to join the team.

The WI ballroom competition was the following week. Bill and Ann were over visiting so joined the rest of the family in the audience to watch Aggie's big moment. The competitors filed out and Aggie appeared in her ballgown accompanied by Peggy in a trouser suit. Peggy took the lead in the foxtrot.

"What is happening?" Gavin asked in confusion. "I thought Eduardo from the hairdressers was Aggie's dance partner?"

"He was, but he kept getting the feeling he was being watched when he would meet Aggie for rehearsal, it made him paranoid...so paranoid that when he heard someone in his garden he set about them with a marching baton and a can of hairspray. It was community Police doing safety checks on peoples gardens and sheds. He's up in court and in disgrace, he refuses to set foot outdoors. Peggy felt so bad that she agreed to be Aggie's partner, but not bad enough to tell her why." Ellie explained as Gavin roared with laughter.

They watched as the pair elegantly swept around the dancefloor and cheered and went mad when they took a bow.

"What would we do without them eh?" asked Kate as she wrapped her arms around Ellie.

"What indeed." Ellie whispered as she watched their antics with happiness in her heart.

The End

Books By This Author

The Arc (Dci Ellie Mcvey Series Book 1)

Death On The Dream (Dci Ellie Mcvey Series Book 2)

Explosion In The Arts (Dci Ellie Mcvey Series Book 3)

Double Trouble (Dci Ellie Mcvey Series Book 4)

Murder In The Mews (Dci Ellie Mcvey Series Book 5)

About The Author

Ja Rainbow

J.A. Rainbow is an author based in Glasgow. She lives there with her wife and two dogs. She has always enjoyed mystery novels, especially ones that mix light-hearted humour along with drama. Although not a native Glaswegian, she is proud to live in the city and to show it off whenever she can.

Praise For Author

I loved this book. Great M.C. Great back up cast. Lovely to see Glasgow portrayed so well with all the places I know so well.The story line was well thought out got my heart rate up. Looking forward to the follow up books. Highly recommend

- THE ARC

Wonderful book I really enjoyed the twists and characters. Full of laughs and tears at times can't wait to start the next one

- DEATH IN THE DREAM

Wow just amazing. What a great book. I feel as if I ran all over Glasgow half the night. Every time I thought it was all settled we were off at and in again.This author wrote two great books before this but she has taken off like a rocket with this one. I loved this book.I need to go back and read all the bits I missed reading so fast. Thank goodness there is more books I don't want to leave these people yet.Thank you very much for a fantastic book.Oh I highly highly recommend.lol.

- EXPOSION IN THE ARTS

Love the way the crimes all have a different slant from book to book. They are not just a formulaic repeat of what went before. They certainly keep your interest and the humour made me laugh out loud. I love the romance and loving family in the background and how Peggy is often able to provide a bit of help on the sidelines. Looking forward to the next in the series.

- DOUBLE TROUBLE

I have spent all weekend in a reading marathon reading all five books one after another. This is a really
great series. I loved everything about it. The books just got better and better.So looking forward to the next instalment. Highly recommend.

- MURDER IN THE MEWS

www.ingramcontent.com/pod-product-compliance
Lightning Source LLC
Chambersburg PA
CBHW050517160726
48003CB00001B/351